AGE OF END:
VIGO'S LAMENT

AGE OF END: VIGO'S LAMENT
by Chris Yee

ISBN 978-0-9973536-5-5

Cover designed by Rebecca Frank
http://RebeccaFrank.design

Published by To The Moon Publishing
www.tothemoonpublish.com

ONE

SIMON LIT THE fuse of the bomb, wandered over to the evacuation pod, and propped it up against the glass. He backed away and crossed his arms. A smirk crept across his face.

Evacuation Pod A will eject in ten seconds.

He watched the group inside panic. The fuse burned down, and a loud blast violently shook the floor. The air was shrouded with smoke and fire. He kept his eyes on the smoke, waiting for it to clear. As the pod became visible, he saw the glass was intact. Only a small crack formed at the base.

"Goddamn it!" he yelled.

Evacuation Pod A ejecting.

Vince and his group shot away from the Spire and out of Simon's reach. A strong gust of wind blew through the opening before a door slid down and sealed the hole.

Simon yelled again, this time directly at the man to his right. He drew his gun, aimed at the man's head, and pulled the trigger. The other men flinched as the body fell lifeless to the floor. He lowered his gun and shrugged, nudging Greene's body with his foot. "At least we killed this bastard. Let's go. We still have work to do."

He walked to Greene's desk and slammed his fist against a big red button. The blaring alarm went silent. Next, he grabbed the microphone and pushed the blue button next to it.

"Attention, everyone. This is Simon, speaking from Greene's office. As you may have guessed, Greene is dead. I'm looking at his bloody corpse right now. Your leader is gone. His empire is over, and a new age has begun. I will free all of his prisoners. You are free to go as long as you don't get in my way."

He hit the button again and put down the microphone. He stood up, rubbed his chin, and snapped his finger at his men. "Kill everyone wearing a Spire uniform."

"Yes sir," they said all at once, marching out of the room.

He looked up at the screen above Greene's desk to see a map of the Spire. He took the controls and rotated the three-dimensional image, zooming in to get a better look. His eyes searched the layout of each level.

"There," he said, pointing to a blinking light on the map. "The cell room. That's where he's keeping them. Now, let's see if I have control from up here." He fiddled around a bit more. "Here it is." He pressed a button.

Power to the cell room has been disabled. Locks deactivated.

"Good work, sir," Jonah said, walking up behind him, holding his turtle mug.

"Christ, Jonah. You and your tea."

Next, Simon looked for the safe rooms. "Let's make it a little easier for my troops." He scrolled through and pushed another button.

Power to the safe rooms has been disabled. Locks deactivated. Evacuation pods deactivated.

As Simon closed the directory, he noticed an intriguing log hidden among the rest of the files. "What is this?" he asked with interest.

"It looks like a record of where everyone in the building goes," Jonah said, after taking a small sip of tea. "They must be scanning people when they walk through doors."

Simon chuckled. "That sounds like something Greene would do. That prick never cared about privacy." There were thousands of employees listed, each with entries dating back fifty years prior. "Ha! Greene's in here too. Let's see where you were before I killed you."

Reading through the logs, something struck his curiosity. When they broke through the third wall, Greene was up in his office, but he did not go to the evacuation pod like Simon would have expected. Instead, he went down to the floor below. *Level 149*. He went to one of the labs and stayed there for four minutes and thirty-two seconds. There was a small camera icon at the bottom of the screen. Simon clicked it and activated video footage from the lab.

The top corner read *Vitality Lab No. 88*. There was no sound, just the image of Greene, huddled over a desk. His actions were hidden in shadow. A small girl stood next to him, tugging on the sleeve of his shirt. She seemed frightened, probably from the flashing lights of the alarm. Greene finished up what he was doing and turned around to pick her up. He ran out of the door, leaving behind a closed book and a pen sitting beside each other on the desk.

Simon stared at the book. "What are you up to?" He zoomed in on the book, but the image was too blurred. He shut off the screen and stood up. "We're going down there," he said to Jonah. "We're going to find out what he was doing with that book."

"It has to be something good," Jonah replied. "If that's the first place he went after we broke in, it must be important to him."

Simon bent over to search Greene's pockets. "Exactly. But what is more important than getting out alive? He had plenty of time to get to that evacuation pod, but he chose not to." He found a plastic key card. It had the City emblem imprinted on the front.

Jonah shrugged. "My guess is as good as yours."

Simon stuck the key card in his pocket and walked towards the door. "Come on, you're coming with me."

They left the room and strolled down the hall with a squad of Crowns following. They entered the elevator and pressed *Level 149*. His men remained silent, out of both fear and respect. They were honored to be a part of this revolution, but they were also nervous that Simon would lose his mind and shoot them in the head in a fit of rage.

The doors slid open, and they walked to the lab area. Simon stopped in front of No. 88. "It's this one," he said, reaching for the key card. He pulled it out of his pocket, but the door slid open on its own. A pleasant voice chimed through the speakers. *Welcome, Mr. Greene.* The lights flickered on, revealing a desk against the back wall.

"So this is what a testing lab looks like," Jonah said, exploring the room. There was a hint of fascination in his voice.

"That's right. This is where it all happens."

"It's strange. I expected it to be more, you know, like a lab. This is just a normal room. It's like an office."

"I agree, it's not what I expected, but that doesn't really matter, I suppose."

"Wait," Jonah said, pointing to a sign hanging from the ceiling. "Operation room? That sounds a little more appropriate."

They walked to the door underneath the sign, and it slid open. The room was sterile and white all over. White tiled walls and floors, complete with large glaring lights from above. Everything glowed with an uncomfortable feeling of cleanliness.

"Now this is what I expected," Simon said.

"Jeez. I feel like I shouldn't bring tea in here. It might stain the white."

"No one's going to care. I certainly don't. Spill away to your heart's content."

"No, no. Someone went through a lot of trouble to clean this room." He went back out and placed his mug on the desk, before returning. "Besides, we might want to use this room. If we dirty it up now, we'll just have to clean it up later."

Simon chuckled. "Why would we use this room? It's a testing room. It's where labbies do experiments on innocent people. That's its only purpose. We have no use for a room like this."

Jonah shrugged. "You never know." He walked around and studied the operating table in the middle. Stacks of machines sat next to it, with wires tangled up at the base. A large tank of compressed gas sat next to them. On the side, was a crudely drawn man sleeping. "Knockout gas?" he asked.

Simon watched him. "Why are you so interested in that stuff? Planning an operation?"

"I'm just fascinated by the resources they have. This is so much more than what we have. Now we have access to all of Greene's stuff. Doesn't that excite you?"

"Not in the slightest. What *does* excite me is that book on the desk out there. Greene thought it was important enough to come down here in the middle of a large-scale attack. Whatever's in that book has to be good."

He left the operation room and returned to the desk. The book and pen sat on top, just as Greene had left them in the video, right next to Jonah's turtle mug. He picked it up and ran his fingers over the leather bound cover. Words were printed in gold ink. *Monitor Journal: Project Monika.*

He looked back through the door to see Jonah pushing buttons on the machines, and shook his head. "What a moron," he said, looking back down.

He flipped to the first page and began to read. As he made his way through the entries, he was caught off guard. It was one of the most unexpected things he had ever read in his life. He clapped the book closed and called over to Jonah. "Hey, quit messing around and get out here. We have work to do."

Jonah came out and immediately grabbed his tea. After a nice long sip, he looked at the book. "What did you find?"

Simon handed it over. "You're going to want to read this."

TWO

ELLA AND RUPERT paddled. The waves crashed against the raft, rocking them up and down. Alan shook Vince's shoulder, trying to snap him out of whatever daze he had fallen into, but he just stared at the horizon with lifeless eyes. Charlotte and Izzy nestled in the corner. Izzy clung to her arm with a solid grip, and Charlotte wrapped her other arm around the girl's back to hold her close. Fred sat at the center of the raft, gently pecking at the stump where her wing used to be. The Spire was far behind them, barely visible anymore. Just a speck in the distance.

Alan waved his hand in front of Vince's face one last time and gave up. "Do you think we're almost there?" he asked as he turned to look ahead.

"I doubt it," Ella said. "It's only been a day. Remember how long it took to get out here in the first place?"

"And that's when you had Barnabus' motorized boat," Charlotte pointed out. "At least for part of the trip. We don't have one of those. We still have a long way to go."

Alan shook his head, disappointed. "Damn, I'm getting pretty hungry."

"You'll have to wait until we get home," Rupert said. "Or maybe we'll get lucky and run into that abandoned boat again. You can raid the pantry."

Alan held his stomach as it rumbled. "Psshh! Like that'll ever happen." Right on cue, an object appeared on the horizon. He stood up and peered ahead. The shape slowly formed into what looked like a boat. He chuckled and slapped his knee. "What are the chances of that?"

Charlotte watched the shape carefully as it became clearer. It was unquestionably a boat, but its shape was growing quickly. Too quickly. This boat was not stationary. It was moving towards them, and fast. It was not abandoned either. Three men stood out on the front deck, all wearing the same uniform.

"Those are Greene's military uniforms," she said. "They must be Greene's soldiers, heading back to The City." She squinted saw the man in front looking back at her. He was pointing towards them and yelling something to the others. The three men gathered at the front and drew guns at the same time. Charlotte flinched. "And those are Greene's weapons." She pointed to the guns at the middle of the raft. "I don't think they're looking to have a friendly conversation. Quick, get your guns!"

Ella, Rupert, and Alan scrambled towards their bags and pulled out the weapons they had picked up from the Spire. Ella tossed a rifle to Charlotte, who caught it and left Izzy's side to point her sights at the boat. Izzy curled up in a ball and rocked back and forth with the waves. Vince did not move. He stared off as if nothing was happening.

Charlotte held up her hand. "Don't fire yet. They're out of range. We can't afford to waste bullets. From what I see, we outnumber them, but they almost certainly have more firepower. We need to make every shot count. Be careful. These men were trained by Greene. They are highly specialized and extremely dangerous."

"Well, duh," Alan said.

They focused their aim, waiting for the boat to come closer. Waiting for Charlotte's order to fire. A hard thud came from behind, near the back of the raft. They swung around to see Izzy sprawled out, her body shaking uncontrollably.

"What's happening?" Alan said, dropping his gun and trotting over. "What's wrong with her?"

They looked to Charlotte, who shrugged, glancing back and trying to keep her sights on the boat at the same time. "She's having some sort of seizure!"

The girl was nearing the edge of the raft, but Alan grabbed her arm before she went over. "What do I do?"

"Just make sure she doesn't fall off," Rupert said. "The three of us will deal with these men."

Alan held her shoulders down. "What if she's dying? We have to do something!"

Ella stared down the sights of her gun. "If we don't deal with Greene's men, we're *all* dead. Just keep her still. We'll help when we can."

Alan shook his head, frustrated. He looked to Vince, who was still in a daze. "Damn it, Vince! Now would be a great time for you to snap out of it."

Charlotte raised her hand again. "Get ready. Fire!"

Three shots echoed in rapid succession. One of Greene's men screamed in pain and toppled into the water. His body skipped along the surface and sank below the waves. The other men watched their comrade fall and turned around to shout something. The boat slowed to a stop and two more men replaced him, both with very large guns.

"Crap!" Charlotte yelled. "I guess we *don't* outnumber them." She looked back at Alan, who was still struggling with Izzy's tremors. "Keep at it, but stay low." She whipped around to Ella and Rupert. "You two stay low as well. And don't stop firing. I'll be right back." She dropped her rifle and dove head first into the water.

"What the hell is she doing?" Alan yelled, dropping down to his stomach. His question was muted by the thunderous gunfire. He supposed they did not have an answer for him anyway. He looked to Vince, who was still kneeling upright as bullets whizzed by. "Get down, you idiot! You're going to get yourself killed!" He reached over to pull him down, but Vince would not budge. "Fine, stay up! But if you get shot, don't even think about draining me!"

Charlotte popped out of the water behind the boat and grabbed onto the ladder. The men had not noticed that she left the raft. They were completely focused on Ella and Rupert. Charlotte climbed up the ladder and walked along the deck. She crouched low to keep out of sight and hugged the wall as she slid down the corridor. She poked her head up to see through the window above her. There were two more men, both hunched over, arguing over a map on the table. She lowered back down and slowly made her way to the door, peeking around the corner. Another scream of pain came from the front of the boat, followed by a splash. Two down, five to go.

Charlotte pulled her head back just as the men turned around. "What's going on out there?" one of them said. His voice was low and raspy. "Those idiots really can't handle a few stragglers?"

Charlotte pressed up against the wall as footsteps approached the door, hoping he wouldn't see her. He came through the door and turned the other way, towards the front of the boat. She immediately sprung from the wall and followed behind him, drawing a knife from her belt. Once she was close enough, she wrapped her arm around his mouth and pushed the knife into his jugular. She pulled it out, and blood spurted out like a fountain of crimson rain. She held him upright as he fought off death, and laid his body on the ground once he lost. Three down, four to go.

She grabbed the rifle strapped to his chest and turned the corner, shooting the man who was still pondering over the map. His head exploded, splattering chunks of brain against the wall. Four down. She ran across the room and knelt down by his body, keeping her gun pointed at the door.

The gunfire from the front had stopped. There was silence. She waited, finger leaning against the trigger. A man came running into the room, his gun raised up and ready to shoot. Charlotte pulled her finger and watched the bullet push him back towards the railing. He toppled over and fell into the water. Five down. There was another bout of silence, this one tenser than the last. A mirror poked out around the corner. Charlotte shot it immediately. The glass shattered into tiny shards. The man dropped the handle and screamed in agony.

"My eyes!" He stumbled into the room and fell to his knees. Jagged pieces of mirror jutted from his face. He brought his hands up to cover the pain, but only managed to press the glass in further. She put a bullet through his hand and into his skull. Six down. One more.

She waited for the last man to enter, but he remained outside. He had learned from his six other friends. A small metal ball rolled through the door and bumped up against one of the bodies. A thick dark smoke sprayed out from the sides and quickly filled the room. Two more balls rolled in shortly after and did the same. She swung the gun strap across her chest, covered her mouth with her shirt, and quickly made her way towards the door.

Before she reached the door, she stopped at the soldier with glass embedded in his face. She wrapped her arms around his chest and lugged his body up. He was heavy, but not too heavy. She held him up by the straps on his uniform and ran through the door. She felt the force of bullets hit her meat shield. Blood splattered along walls with each shot. She moved forward with surprising speed, closing in on her shooter. With every shot, even more blood sprayed. One bullet went straight through the body and grazed the side of her neck. After the barrage of fire, she finally heard the sound she was waiting for.

Click

She threw the body forward and charged at the soldier, grasping the knife in her hand. With great force and unthinkable speed, she plunged the knife into his forehead. She pulled it out and cleaned off the blood as the body fell to the ground. Seven down.

With the boat cleared out, she took a moment to catch her breath, leaning against the railing and wiping the blood and sweat off her face. Her chest puffed in and out as she sucked in a lungful of air. Once she was calm, she got up and headed to the front of the boat, where she saw her friends on the raft. Ella and Rupert lowered their guns. Fred squawked a cheery screech and hopped up and down. Alan still knelt over Izzy, whose seizure had finally ended. Vince was exactly the same as before. She waved to them. "It's safe! The boat's clear! Come on over!"

They paddled over and climbed onboard, walking around and examining the four bodies on the ground.

Alan gazed at Charlotte with amazement. "Where did you learn how to fight like that?"

"The same place they did," she said as she nudged a body with her foot. "I went through Greene's training program, although that was a good while ago now. It looks like they may have softened up a bit. These guys didn't put up much of a fight."

"Or you just put up one hell of a good one," Alan said, staring down at the blood trickling from the soldier's neck.

Charlotte pointed to Ella and Rupert. "You two didn't do half bad. Impressive, considering you have no combat experience." Her eyes went to Izzy, who was now perfectly fine. "Are you okay?"

Izzy nodded.

"What happened over there? Have you had these seizures before?"

She nodded again. "They're normal. I have them all the time. Daddy said it's a condition I have."

"What kind of condition?"

Izzy shrugged.

"We'll talk about that later," Ella said, looking around at the condition of the boat. "Right now, it looks like we have one of those motorized boats you were talking about, Charlotte."

"Yes we do," Charlotte said. "I'll go see if I can get it running. Greene has so many models of these boats, you never know what to expect. This could be a new model I'm not familiar with."

Alan's face lit up. "Do you think it has a pantry?"

"Most likely. A pantry is pretty standard for these things."

"I'm starving!" he said, running off with excitement.

"We should get rid of these bodies," Rupert said. "Just dump them in the water, I suppose."

Charlotte nodded. "That's the easiest way."

Ella, Rupert, and Charlotte gathered the bodies and threw them overboard. When they were done, they followed Alan's lead and explored the rest of the boat.

The pantry was on the first floor, just before the staircase, and was smaller than the one on the other boat. It was the size of a small closet, but was still packed with boxes and cans of food, and jugs of drinking water sat on the floor under the shelves. They found Alan crouched in the corner, stuffing his face with salted crackers and drinking directly from one of the jugs. He paused briefly, looking back at them, and held up the box to offer some crackers. They took the box and passed it around. Alan grabbed a fresh one and opened it for himself.

With their stomachs satisfied, they continued exploring the boat. The layout was similar to Barnabus' boat, but smaller, and had two bedrooms instead of one. Each bedroom held two sets of bunk beds.

"It's weird," Ella said as she studied them. "For a boat designed for eight people, this is much smaller than the other one."

Charlotte nodded. "This must be a newer model. Greene has been pushing for efficiency. In the labs, he emphasized the importance of low cost. I guess that carried over to boat designs too."

"And the cell room," Alan added. "Man, those cells were small."

Ella nodded in agreement. "The test subjects looked miserable behind those bars."

"*I* was miserable," Alan said, "and I was only in there for a day."

"Well, I guess we don't have to worry about that anymore," Charlotte said. "Now that Simon's in control of the Spire, I'm pretty sure those cells won't be used anymore."

Next, they found the control room. The set up was completely different than the last. Charlotte looked at the control board and smiled. "It looks different, but I can drive this."

Rupert examined the board with a puzzled face. "Good, because we would never figure this out. It's far more complicated than the other one."

"I've used this set-up before," she said. "It looks overwhelming, but it's really quite easy once you know what you're doing."

Alan smirked. "We'll just leave the driving to you."

THREE

THEY DROVE THE boat up on the grainy sands of the beach and headed back into the cave. A strong stench filled the air as they walked deeper into the hollow caverns. The scent conjured unpleasant memories. For Rupert, Ella, and Alan, memories of their dear friend Patrick resurfaced, and for Vince, the memory of Saul. The cave had nothing but nightmares to offer, and they were eager to get out as quickly as possible. They turned the corner and saw Barnabus, surrounded by crusted blood and covered in maggots.

"Damn, it stinks in here," Alan said. He turned his head and saw the cage full of dismembered bodies. The flesh had turned to gelatinous goo, and the blood had curdled at the base. A thick swarm of flies surrounded the pile, buzzing furiously as they zipped through the air. He covered his mouth and almost gagged. "And that would be why."

"I almost forgot about this," Ella said.

"Forgot about it? How could you forget about this? I wish I could forget it, but this image is burned into my brain."

Charlotte covered her mouth as well. "I watched this on the monitors. It's far worse in person."

"Of course it is," Alan said, stepping back. "someone really needs to clean this up."

They all glanced at each other, waiting for a volunteer.

"Right," Alan said. "I guess none of us are up to the task. We're not coming back here anyway. It doesn't hurt to leave it. We'll never see it again."

"Let's just move on and get home," Rupert said. "This journey's been long enough as it is."

"We could take the cage," Charlotte said. "It has a motor. We could get to Snow Peak much faster and skip the five-day walk."

Alan took another long look at the pile of blood and guts. It was even worse than the image that was burned into his brain. The bodies were decomposing into a pink mush. "You want us to clean this thing up? No, thank you. I would much rather walk."

"Are you sure? We could save a lot of time. It would easily cut the trip down to two days."

"Do you see what I see? There's no way I'm touching that mess. We're in no rush. We have food and supplies from the boat. We could walk *ten* days for all I care."

Rupert inspected the cage. "If it can really cut down our trip to two days, it may be worth the effort."

"I plan on returning to the City, too," Charlotte said. "I can use it on my trip back."

Ella shrugged. "I just want to be home. If this gets us there faster, I'm all in."

Alan glared at all of them, shocked. "Seriously? You would all rather clean this mess than walk a few extra days? What about you, Vince? Come on, back me up."

Vince stared at the cage, but said nothing.

Alan threw his arms up. "Oh right, Vince has gone mute. Well, that's just great. I guess we're cleaning it then. You guys are nuts."

They got to work and started clearing off the cage. They started with the main pile, scooping layers off with their hands and throwing them aside. The overpowering smell was unbearable. Alan glanced at the bone sticking out in his hands. He dropped it, twisted around and hunched over to barf. The sound made the others cringe.

Ella tried to limit her breathing, but the physical work was demanding. She let in a gigantic breath. The wretched fumes climbed up her nose and entered her lungs. She grew lightheaded and fell to the ground, away from the guts and onto dry dirt.

Rupert tossed the gunk in his hands and ran over to help her. He knelt down by her body. "Ella, are you okay?" She was unconscious. He looked over to Alan, who was kneeling in the corner with his hands pressed against his forehead. He looked back to the pile, which they had barely made a dent on. "This isn't worth it. Let's walk the rest of the way."

Alan spun around. "Thank god. I told you it wasn't worth it, but you wouldn't listen."

"I underestimated the work involved. This is dangerous to our health. Walking may take longer, but it will be calm. After everything we've been through, we need calm."

Charlotte turned after scooping another handful. "Are you sure? We've already started. We're already covered in the stuff. You want to give up now?"

"Christ, Charlotte," Alan said, still hunched over a puddle of his own bile. "Ella's passed out, and I'm sitting in my own fluids. Yes, we would gladly give up."

She sighed. "Okay, I guess we can walk."

Alan stood up. "I'm going back to the beach to wash off first."

"You're going to the ocean to wash?" Rupert said. "It's salt water."

Alan looked up and down his own body. "I'm covered in blood and guts. I think salt water is a bit of an upgrade." He started walking off and pointed to the cage. "I never want to see that cage again. Ever."

FOUR

THEY ARRIVED AT the edge of the woods. After a long walk across the snow plains, they were almost home.

Ella ran ahead of the pack. "I can't wait to see everyone. They must all be so worried."

Alan laughed. "You're really excited."

"And you're not? Tell me you're not eager to see your beautiful wife."

Alan smirked. "Okay I'll admit, I'm kind of excited."

"Kind of?" Ella said. "You should be ecstatic." She jumped in the air and threw her arms up.

"You're right," Alan said. "I should be more excited." He ran up and mimicked Ella's little jump.

"It will be nice to check on Carl," Rupert said. "I know he's in good hands, but that boy can be a handful sometimes."

Ella ran back to Charlotte and Izzy, who were walking side by side. "You two can meet everyone. They're all so nice. They'll welcome you with open arms."

Charlotte smiled. "Thank you. I look forward to meeting them."

Izzy stayed quiet, but held a wide grin.

Alan looked over his shoulder at Vince, who was dragging behind the group and had not said a single word since they left the City. "I hope he's okay."

"He just needs time," Rupert said. "His best friend was killed right in front of him. A friend he's known his entire life. I'm sure he'll open up eventually, but for now, give him his space."

"Right," Ella said. "He might feel like he's lost his only friend, but he hasn't. We're here for him when he needs us." She looked straight ahead and pointed forward. "In the meantime, we march towards Snow Peak, because there's nowhere I'd rather be right now than home."

"How should we break the news to Martha?" Alan asked.

"She's a strong woman," Rupert said, "but she'll be devastated. She truly loved Patrick. She fell apart when he first went missing. It will be tough to tell her, but it must be done. We should tell her together."

"Right," Alan said. "We'll be there to comfort her. She should have friends around when she hears the news."

"Where will *we* stay?" Charlotte asked.

"We have a few empty cabins. We'll fit you in somewhere. You two could stay together. I don't want someone her age staying by herself."

Charlotte pulled Izzy in closer, rubbing her shoulder. "My thoughts exactly."

Rupert smiled. "She seems to like you."

"Of course she likes me," she said jokingly. "What's not to like?"

"I suppose not much. Either way, I'm glad she's comfortable around you." He bent down to Izzy's level. "You're going to stay with us. How does that sound?"

Izzy blushed and hid behind Charlotte.

"Oh, come on Izzy," Charlotte said. "Rupert's pretty much the nicest person you'll ever meet. You don't need to be afraid of him."

Rupert chuckled. "Ah, it's okay. I'm a big guy with a bushy beard. I'd scare myself too."

She patted Izzy's head. "She'll warm up to you soon enough. To all of you. She's just been through a lot."

"We all have," Rupert said. "I think this Snow Peak reunion will be good for us. It will lighten our spirits."

Fred fluttered on Rupert's shoulder.

He took her in his arms and stroked her feathers. "Calm down girl. There's nothing to worry about. We're almost home."

She ignored his words and wriggled from his grip, popping out and falling to the snow.

"What's gotten into you?" he said, watching her wobble ahead of the group. "She must still be adjusting to her injury. It will take some time for her to get used to only having one wing."

Ella tilted her head. "Are you sure that's what it is? She doesn't seem herself. It's true, she's been acting different ever since we rescued her, but if anything she's been calmer. This is different. Something's bothering her."

"And what would that be?" Alan asked.

Rupert shrugged. "I don't know, but hopefully seeing some familiar faces will calm her down. Maybe she's just excited to see everyone."

"Maybe," Ella said.

Rupert looked ahead. "I should probably go get her." He trotted forward to catch up.

Alan glanced at Vince again. "Do you think he'll stick around?"

"I don't know," Ella said. "He's done what he set out to do. Greene's dead and the tests are over. Obviously, he's welcome to stay if he wants, but he's been traveling his whole life with a purpose. Now that his purpose is gone, I don't know what he'll do."

"And Saul's death doesn't help," Charlotte said. "I think he was hoping to go through this with Saul. Together they would figure out what to do next, but now he's left alone."

"He's not alone," Ella said. "He just doesn't realize it."

"He's a smart guy," Alan said. "He'll catch on."

There was a scream from up ahead. "No!" Their heads popped up. It was Rupert's voice. Their casual walk turned to a nervous jog.

"Something's wrong," Ella said.

"What?" Alan asked.

"I don't know. I just have a bad feeling. Something happened in Snow Peak while we were gone."

Alan flashed a look of concern and ran faster. Ella, Charlotte, and Izzy followed. They emerged from the woods and saw what had prompted the scream. It was carnage. Blood. Bodies. Dead. Scattered along the road. Deep stains of red drenched the white snow. Pools of crimson. Bodies were splayed along the center of the road, littered with bullets.

Rupert was kneeling over a body, weeping. They walked up behind him to see who it was. He turned his head and moved aside to reveal the corpse of a child. It was Carl. Blood trailed from the hole in his neck. Ella looked at Carl's face, and tears flooded her eyes. She looked down at her feet. She couldn't bear the sight. Then a thought invaded her mind.

"No," she whispered. She looked up and searched through the bodies. "Mother? Where are you? Mother!"

Alan watched her dig through the bodies, searching for her mother, until the same realization entered his mind as well. His wife, Melinda. He ran frantically along the other side. "Melinda? Honey! Please don't do this. Please."

Rupert remained on his knees next to Carl's body. He could not move. He could not speak. He could only watch as his friends dug through loved ones. Ella found her mother, shot through the head. She held her close and wept. Alan found his wife, shot three times in the chest. He leaned in and kissed her forehead. Everyone they knew, everyone in Snow Peak, was dead.

Charlotte watched from the side as her new friends grieved the brutal death of their village. She pulled Izzy closer, shielding her innocent eyes from the gruesome scene. There was nothing she could do to help. Any words, any actions, would just upset them. So she stayed silent, watching in sorrow.

"How could this happen?" Rupert asked. "Who would do such a thing."

"It was Greene," Vince said, emerging from the woods. His first spoken words since they left the Spire. "Soldiers were acting under Greene's orders."

Alan wiped the tears from his face. "Greene's dead."

"It was before he died. A few days prior. He sent troops and took Snow Peak hostage. They were ordered to kill everyone if he didn't report in at the start of every day. It was his way of keeping us in line. Making sure we didn't kill him. The day he died, they were all doomed."

"Charlotte?" Alan asked, looking at her with accusing eyes.

"She didn't know," Vince said. "Saul and I were the only ones."

Ella's faced grew red. "You knew about this, and you didn't say anything? We were going to kill Greene that day! If Simon hadn't done it, one of us would have! How could you not tell us our loved ones were in danger? Our families? Everyone we know? How could you do that?"

Alan shook his head and ran off to his cabin, slamming the door behind him.

Vince looked down at the snow. "I am sorry. I was reckless. I thought we could outsmart him. I now see that I should have told you from the start."

Ella stood up and marched towards him. "Yeah you should have told us! That's what friends do. They tell each other when their families are in danger." Fiery rage engulfed her face. She walked up to him and swung her fist right into his cheek.

Vince fell over. Blood flew from his nose and mouth. Rupert jumped to his feet and held Ella back. Vince held up his hand. "It's okay, Rupert. Let her." Rupert released her, and she stumbled forward. She glared into his eyes with intense anger. Her breaths were short, and tears ran down her cheeks. Without a word, she turned around and walked away. She knocked on the door to Alan's cabin and let herself in.

Vince turned to Rupert. His face was firm. Fred was hunched over on his shoulder, looking at the scattered bodies and quietly chirping to herself. Rupert walked up and patted his shoulder, averting his eyes, before turning around to join the others.

Charlotte approached from behind, holding Izzy in her arms. "They'll come around. You were put in a difficult situation, and you chose to go for Greene. I don't blame you. I had no idea he was capable of such awful things. He was just as bad as Simon."

"No," Vince said. "He was worse than Simon. Simon doesn't hide who he is. Everyone knows he's crazy, but they follow him anyway. Greene hid behind a mask. He lied to people to gain their trust, and when it was convenient for him, he cut them loose. Like us. He was just like Simon, but he kept it secret."

"That's not the only thing he kept secret," she said, looking down at Izzy. "How long did your father keep you up there, honey?"

The girl shied away.

Charlotte bobbed her up and down. "It's okay. You can tell us."

"I don't know," she said softly. "For as long as I can remember."

Charlotte brushed the hair out of Izzy's eyes. "You've been up in the Spire for your whole life?"

She nodded. "Dad said it wasn't safe to leave. He said people wouldn't understand."

"Understand what?"

She shrugged.

Vince tilted his head to catch the girl's eyes. "Who is your mother?"

She shrugged again. "Dad never told me."

"Why would he hide his child from the world? What wouldn't people understand?"

"Maybe he thought it would hurt his image," Charlotte suggested. "It would make him look soft. He had no time for love. No time for a wife or daughter. Whoever her mother is, he cut *her* loose as well."

"And she never said anything?"

"Greene must have paid her off."

"But he kept Izzy?"

She looked at the girl's big puffy eyes. "No one could give up this cute little face. Not even Greene." She poked Izzy's nose with the tip of her finger. "She's as sweet as a gumdrop."

"Okay," Vince said. "So, what was he waiting for? Surely he wasn't planning on keeping her a secret forever."

"Your guess is as good as mine. But that doesn't matter. The past is the past. What *does* matter is what we do next. We can either stay here." She surveyed the area, cringing at the sight of death wherever she looked. "Or we can go back to the City. You already know my vote."

"We'll see what the others think, but we should let them calm down first. Before we go anywhere, we should have a proper burial for their friends and family. I met all of these people. They were good human beings. They deserve a little dignity in the afterlife. It will be good for the others as well."

Charlotte nodded and studied Vince's face. "How are *you* doing? You haven't said much since we left. Are you okay?"

"I'll be fine."

"Are you sure? Because if you want to talk about Saul, I'm here to listen."

He turned away. "Don't worry about me. There are more important things to do right now." He walked towards the bodies and stood over them. "We'll take the night to rest, and tomorrow, we'll bury them. We'll hold a formal ceremony to show respect for those who have died. There will be no talk about future plans until after the burial."

Charlotte nodded. "Of course."

Vince waved her on. "Go check in on them and make sure they're okay. I'll start digging."

She looked at the line of bodies. "There are so many of them. It will take you all night."

"I want to do it. I owe them," he said, head down. "They're right. I should have told them. If I did, these people might still be alive. This won't make up for it, but it's a start."

"I'll put in a good word for you," she said, walking past him. She covered Izzy's eyes as they passed by the bodies.

Vince took a deep breath and surveyed the land. A night of digging would be exhausting, but it was something he felt he must do. It was something he *wanted* to do. He walked to the supply shed to fetch a shovel. After everything he put up with over the last two

hundred years, one cold night of digging did not sound
so bad.

FIVE

TRISH BUZZED UNIT Three of Building Twenty-Six and turned around to watch the street while she waited. Ever since the Spire fell, the streets were more crowded than ever. Former Spire workers roamed about with no place to go. They were forced to sleep on the outside. Trish was one of the lucky ones. She did not have any family, but was fortunate enough to know Warren and his wife, Dana. They welcomed her into their home with open arms.

Not many home dwellers were willing to help the homeless, now that Greene was dead and Simon was in charge. Anyone from the Spire or associated with Greene in any way now had to watch their back. Trish was convinced that Simon was on a mission to eliminate every last one of them. Now that he was in control of the Spire and the surveillance systems, that mission was hauntingly reachable. She spun around to buzz again, but the door swung open before she could.

It was Dana. "Trish, please come in." She leaned in to offer a hug and then led her up the long flight of stairs. "Sorry to keep you waiting. Warren has his hands full with dinner at the moment."

"No worries. I think waiting outside for a few minutes is the least of anyone's problems nowadays."

"How bad is it out there?"

"Pretty bad. And it's getting worse."

Dana shook her head. "There's nowhere for anyone to go. Everyone's too afraid of Simon."

They passed unit two and twisted around with the staircase. "*I'm* afraid of Simon. Aren't you?"

Dana shrugged. "I suppose."

"I hear the news stories from the Eastern District. He's been attacking neighborhoods. Wiping out anyone who's ever worked for Greene."

"They say he's looking for a girl. I don't know who this girl is, but she's the reason for all of this madness."

Trish lowered her head. "Yes, I've heard that too. He's never going to find her, though."

They reached unit three and Dana opened the door to a room filled with a fresh garlic scent. "She's out there somewhere. They're bound to find her eventually."

"No," Trish whispered to herself. "They won't."

"What are you two going on about?" Warren said from around the corner.

Dana entered the kitchen and pecked a kiss on his cheek. "We're talking about that girl Simon's looking for."

He shook his head. "I don't understand why that girl is so goddamn important." He looked to Trish. "You got the vegetables?"

She handed over a bag. "Chopped up and ready to go."

"Perfect timing." He poured the chopped vegetables in and stirred. The pan sizzled with an alluring scent. "I've seen the posters blowing around the streets. There are so many of them. Is the girl really worth all of this trouble?"

"She must be," Dana said. "Otherwise, he would let it go."

"We don't even know who she is," he said. "She's a mystery girl. What, is she like Simon's daughter or something?"

Trish hesitated and decided not to respond.

"Whoever she is, I hope they find her soon. Too many people are dying because of her."

"Amen," Warren said, pouring the veggies onto a plate, next to a pile of chicken and rice. "Let's eat."

They carried the food to the dining room and sat around the table. Trish scooted her chair up, admiring the food. "I'm starving. Everything looks wonderful. You've really outdone yourself, Warren."

"That's my man," Dana said. "He may be getting old, but his cooking only gets better."

"Who's getting old?" Warren said jokingly.

"Oh come on, honey. You're not fooling anyone. Those hairs are turning gray whether you like it or not."

They laughed before digging into the food, piling large servings onto individual plates. They were so hungry that they took a break from conversation to enjoy the food.

A few bites in, Trish sipped some water and turned to Warren. "So what were you going on about this morning? You said something about a ceremony."

"Ah yes. The ceremony. In light of everything that's happened recently, I think it's a good idea to have a gathering. A way to honor those that we've lost the day the Spire fell. A way to honor Victor Greene."

"It's a good idea," Dana said, taking Warren's hand in hers. "These last few days have been rough. Many have lost people close to them. They need a way to mourn.

This will be a good way for people to support each other."

"Right," Warren said. "And it will give us a chance to acknowledge Victor Greene as the great man he was. He helped so many people. He made the City a better place. You of all people should know. You worked closely with him every day. That's why I want you to speak at the ceremony."

"Speak?"

"Yes. Nothing too complicated. Say something inspiring. They need to hear from someone who truly knew the man. They need words of hope."

Trish considered his request. The ceremony was a good idea, but she was not much of a public speaker. "How many people will there be?"

"It's hard to say, but there's been a lot of initial interest."

Trish peered out the window, watching the people wander the streets. "Hmm."

"It will be easy. Your words don't need to be life changing. Just say something upbeat. Some of these people are at their worst, and you worked so closely with Mr. Greene. Anything coming from your mouth will cheer them up."

After some thought, Trish nodded. "Okay. I think I can do that."

"Great," Warren said, jumping out of his seat with excitement. "The people really need this ceremony. The City is at its lowest. The Spire falling was the worst thing that could have happened. Simon's too crazy to be in charge."

"I blame Vincent Vigo and Saul Shepherd," Trish said. "Heroes of the Spire? They're not heroes. They're traitors. Greene gave them everything. He trusted them, and they stabbed him in the back. It puzzles me why they would ever choose to work with Simon."

"Because that's what traitors do," Dana said. "It's impossible to pick their minds. Some people just do bad things."

"That's right," Warren said. "And we can't change what they did to Greene, or what Simon did to the Spire, but we *can* change the future of the City."

Trish squinted. "Oh, so that's really why you're holding this ceremony."

"Correct. Don't get me wrong, we will honor Mr. Greene. We will give him the respect he deserves. But this is the perfect opportunity to fire up the people. You'll get up there and say whatever you have to say. They'll be so inspired that they'll want to rip Simon from his throne. Once you're done speaking, I'll take a list of recruits. Volunteers to join me in storming the Spire. With enough people, I know we can take it back."

"How? Do you have a plan?"

"We'll come up with something. The walls are already down, so it should be as easy as walking through the front doors."

"It can't possibly be that easy. He'll have guards everywhere."

"True, but not as many as you would think. You've seen the news. He's got his forces sweeping the Eastern District and they only seem to be expanding. I'm willing to bet his guards in the Spire are limited."

Trish scooped up the last bits of veggies from her plate and popped them in her mouth. "That's one hell of a chance to take. What if you're wrong?"

"Then I'm wrong, but at least we put up a fight. Sitting around won't get us anywhere. If we wait too long, his troops will bleed over from the Eastern district and make their way over here. Once that happens, we don't stand a chance."

"It sounds risky," Dana said, "but it's the only shot we have. We can't continue to live in fear. You said it yourself. Simon is on a mission to wipe out anyone connected to the Spire. If we don't do something soon, we're as good as dead."

Trish peered out the window once more. She watched the people sitting on the streets without a home. Warren was right. If they did not do something, they would all die.

"Okay," she said. "I'll do my best. When I'm done with my speech, they'll be lining up to fight."

Warren smiled. "Good. Now who wants dessert?"

SIX

RUPERT WOKE UP to blinding sunlight peeking through the cabin window. He had fallen asleep on the floor beside the bed. Ella and Alan lay next to him. Charlotte and Izzy shared the bed, snuggling close together. Fred was perched at the head of the bed frame. The smell of the wood panels filled his nostrils. The scent was comforting after their long absence. Outside he heard the sound of metal, wedging into loose dirt. He pressed his hands to his face and rubbed his eyes. Despite the hardwood floor, he had gotten a surprisingly refreshing night of sleep. It was nice to sleep in a place away from the Spire.

He got to his feet, making sure not to wake the others, and tiptoed to the window. He glanced outside to see

Vince digging a shovel into the ground. Dozens of holes were lined up along the side of the road. The bodies were no longer scattered about, but instead, were each carefully placed beside a hole. Rupert smiled. He stepped outside and quietly shut the door behind him. The brisk air hit his skin. It would take some time to adjust from the warm climate of the City. He pulled his coat around himself and stepped into the road.

"This is good," he called out. "They will like this."

Vince looked up and continued digging. "We should respect the dead."

Rupert walked up to one of the holes and glanced inside. "Indeed. These are deep. You must have been at this all night. Take a rest. I'll dig for a bit."

Vince sunk the shovel down. "I'm not tired. But if you really want to help, grab an extra shovel." He pointed to a pile to his right.

Rupert walked over and picked up a shovel. "Is right here good?"

"Move a little further down. They can't be too close. The walls will cave in."

Rupert took a few steps over and pushed his shovel into the ground. "How are you holding up?"

"Don't worry about me. I'm fine."

"Saul was your oldest friend. It's okay to be shaken up. We all are."

Vince threw a shovelful of dirt over his shoulder. "I'm not. He was going to die anyway, even if Simon hadn't shot him. The bullet in his lung would have killed him."

"That doesn't mean you can't be upset about it. You knew him your whole life."

"And for most of that time, I thought he was a psychotic killer."

"But you were wrong. He wasn't. He was a good guy. A decent human being. And he was your friend. You say to respect the dead, but what about Saul?"

Vince stopped digging. "You think I don't respect Saul? Of course I respect him, but that doesn't mean I'm torn up about it. I've watched so many people die in my lifetime. He just adds to the count."

Rupert pointed to the cabin. "Those guys in there, they're a wreck." His voice wavered. "I'm a wreck. We've lost friends. Family. We are not okay. That's why Ella hit you. She knows you had a difficult choice. She doesn't blame you for this. She just has emotions running through her veins. She needed to let them out, so she hit you. That's normal. This," he gestured to Vince, "whatever you're doing, is not normal."

Vince continued digging. "I haven't been normal in two hundred years."

Rupert sighed. "What I'm saying is, it's okay to feel bad. To be depressed. Sad. Lonely. We all go through it, but we don't stuff it down and hide it. We embrace it. And once it passes, because it always does, the good times are that much better. If you let it fester, only more grief can come of it."

Vince stopped digging again to glare at Rupert. "Trust me. I'm fine."

Rupert shook his head. "Okay then."

The cabin door squeaked open, and Alan stepped out. Ella, Charlotte, and Izzy followed. Fred wobbled along Alan's feet as he stepped through the snow. They wandered over with curious looks. Alan peered at the holes and then at the people lying next to them.

They were all familiar faces. A neighbor. A friend. A loved one. Martha. Horace. Mary. Tamara. Carl. Melinda. Melinda's face was as beautiful as it had always been. Her hands were placed across her chest, covering her wounds. He knelt down and kissed her forehead one last time.

Ella stood next to Vince, staring straight ahead. "What you did was wrong. I want you to know that. When I hit you, I meant it. I wanted to break your nose. I wanted to hurt you because you hurt us. I still want to hurt you." She looked to the hole by her mother's side. "But thank you." She left his side and walked over to join Alan.

A somber grin crept onto Vince's face. He picked up his shovel and continued to dig.

SEVEN

THEY STOOD AROUND Snow Peak's new cemetery, looming over the tombs that were now occupied. Izzy counted the holes and pointed to the one on the end. "There's an extra hole. That one's empty."

Vince shrugged. "I miscounted."

Alan stepped forward. "I suppose we should say something, right? I'll start." He cleared his throat. "Today is a sad day." He paused. "No. Sad is the wrong word. It doesn't capture even a fraction of what I'm feeling right now. Today is a horrendous day. A dreadful day. A tragic day. Yes, I think we can all agree that what happened here was a tragedy. Our friends and family were executed. Shot down. Murdered. However you want to put it. There are many ways to describe what happened, but it doesn't change the outcome. So none of that matters. What *does* matter is what we do next. How we remember them. I will remember Melinda as a loving wife. She was a caring person with a beautiful soul. She was nice to everyone, and she showed endless love for me. Now she is gone, and I will miss her greatly, but I will never stop loving her back." He bent down and drove a wooden plank into the ground. *Melinda Trotter* was carved into it. He bowed his head and stepped back in line with the others.

Next was Ella. "My mother was the best anyone could ask for. She did a wonderful job raising me. She had morals and principles, and she passed them on to me. Her heart of gold would never melt. And whenever things got hard, she was tough as nails. I owe her the world, and I know I can never repay her." Tears trickled from her eyes. "Maybe things could have gone differently." She glanced at Vince and then looked away. "Maybe this whole thing could have been avoided, but now she's gone. I will carry her legacy. I know that would make her happy." She bent down, just like Alan, and planted a plank into the ground. This one read *Tamara Weaver*.

Rupert spoke next. "I want to start by saying that all of these losses are tragic. Every single person here deserves kind words. Every one of them deserves this ceremony. None of them deserved what happened. They did nothing wrong. And we may be tempted to blame certain people." He glanced at Ella, who shot a disgusted look at Vince. "It's natural to do so in times like this, but that's not what we need right now. Now is a time to stick together. To support each other. These last few days have been a crazy mess. We've all lost people. We've all experienced pain and sorrow. Let's not turn against each other in these difficult times. Instead, let's take this time to heal, and help others heal." He turned to Vince. "Vince, this burial was your idea. I think it's only fair you get a chance to speak as well."

Vince raised his head, looking straight into Ella's glare. He turned to the faces of the others, and then to the empty hole at the end. His eyes lingered on the unoccupied tomb, thinking of what to say. Finally, his head sunk and he turned to Rupert. "I have nothing to say."

Rupert studied his face and nodded. "Very well. Charlotte. You never had the pleasure of meeting these wonderful people, but would you like to say something?"

"Yes, of course," Charlotte said. "Though it's true I never met anyone here, I know they were all good people. I have spent most of my life in the Spire. I've watched a lot of people. It was my job to observe people. To study their actions and relationships. Never in my entire career have I seen a group more tightly knit than yours. When I first met you, I knew you were inseparable. You are your own little community. I can imagine the rest of these people were the same way. Rupert is right. In times like these, community is the most valuable thing in the world. I am honored that you have welcomed me into yours."

"And we are honored to have you," Rupert said. "Without you, we never would have escaped the Spire. You risked your life, on more than one occasion, to help us. You've earned your spot in our group."

"Thank you, Rupert."

"Now," Rupert said, bending down and grabbing the plank with Carl's name, "we should place the rest of these names. Then we can talk about what will come next."

They walked up the line and placed the rest of the planks. Each grave had a name. A memorial of the good people of Snow Peak. Their bodies had perished, but their names lived on. They left the extra grave at the end untouched. Rupert headed back towards the warmth of the cabin, and the others followed.

Vince stayed behind, waving them off. "I'll be there in a moment. I just want to do one more thing."

They nodded and went inside.

Vince turned around and looked at all of the graves. His eyes followed down the line, reading each name until he reached the final unnamed tomb. He sauntered over and picked up a blank piece of wood. With his knife, he carefully carved into the surface. When he was done, he held it out at arm's length, and then knelt down to plant it in the ground. He stood up and stared at the empty grave for a moment longer, and then turned around to join the others.

The plank, which was lodged firmly in the ground, read *Saul Shepherd*.

EIGHT

A S VINCE APPROACHED the cabin, his eye caught movement in the woods. He tilted his head and squinted to focus his sight. It was a person. Not just one, but many. Small crowds of people stumbled out of the woods and walked towards the village. Some wore labbie outfits. Long white coats with the City crest embroidered on the chest. Others wore traditional black Spire uniforms, similar to Charlotte's.

Vince trotted to the cabin and flung the door open. "Get out here. There are people coming."

They wandered out with cautious curiosity. The horde of people slowly ambled over. "Who are they?" Alan asked. There was a hint of worry hidden in his voice. "Look at what they're wearing. Is it more of Greene's men?"

"You son of a bitch," Charlotte said, laughing and jumping with joy. "Trevor? You made it out!" She jogged over.

The man in front lifted his head and smiled at the sight of Charlotte. He started jogging as well. "Charlotte!" He met her in the middle and exchanged a warm embrace. "I can't believe you made it out. There was a rumor going around that Greene locked you up."

"He did."

"How did you escape?"

"Vince and Saul broke in and helped me. How did you get out?"

"Just barely. I was in the cosmetic sector, just adding records in my journal like any other day, and then the alarm went off. Even though the second wall was down, Greene was so confident in his last broadcast. I was certain we could handle the attack." He shook his head and laughed nervously. "Man was I wrong! I went to the safe room with everyone else. We've done it so many times lately, it's become somewhat of a routine. Of course, you weren't there. Ever since Vince and Saul came to the City, I haven't seen you at all. I guess Greene kept you busy…or locked up. Either way, I thought you were a goner."

"Thanks for your vote of confidence," Charlotte said, nudging his shoulder.

"Soon after we locked the safe room, Simon made an announcement. He said Greene was dead."

"It's true," she said, looking down at her feet. "I saw his body."

"Up until then, the safe room was pretty, you know, safe. Everyone was after Greene, but once Greene was dead, they focused on the safe rooms. We couldn't just wait to see what happened. Eventually, they would get in. So we turned to the evacuation pods. The thing is, there were too many people. We weren't going to fit. We tried to squeeze as many people as possible, but it became very clear that not everyone would make it out. Some volunteered to stay behind. The rest of us, we drew straws."

"Christ," Charlotte said involuntarily.

"I know. It sucks, but it was the only thing we could think of. I got lucky. I got a spot, but we had to leave five people behind."

"I'm so sorry." She hugged him again. "But I'm glad *you* made it out."

"The entire time I was praying that Simon wouldn't find the fire vacuum button. If he pushed that, we were all goners. It would suck out all the air, and we would suffocate to death. Fortunately, we had enough time to load into the pods. After our three pods had launched, we looked back to see if others were doing the same, but none of the other pods budged. It was just us. We had nowhere to go. We couldn't go back. Not in the middle of that massacre. And we had never crossed the outer wall before. We didn't know what was out here. That's when we saw a raft in the distance. It was just a dot on the horizon, but we saw it."

"That was us," Charlotte said.

Trevor nodded. "We followed you, hoping you would lead us somewhere. Then we heard gunfire, and you disappeared. We lost you. We steered our pods towards the sound and found your abandoned raft. We didn't know what to make of it. So we just kept going forward until we hit land. We were relieved when we saw one of Greene's boats parked up on shore. We figured they could help us, we just had to find them first. We followed the tracks in the snow, hoping to run into them, but instead, we found you."

"That boat was ours," Charlotte said.

Trevor gave a puzzled look. "It's not Greene's men?"

"I guess it is, kind of…It *was*."

Trevor gave an even more puzzled look.

"They attacked us. That was the gunfire you heard. But we kicked them off and took their boat."

"Why in the world would Greene's men attack you?"

"Trevor, have you been living under a rock? Greene had me locked up for treason. Vince and Saul were working with Simon. We're all fugitives. Why wouldn't they attack us?"

Trevor shrugged. "It was just a rumor that you were locked up. I didn't really take it seriously."

"Well, it happened. The Spire has fallen. Greene is dead. The City is probably a mess. So you need to start taking it seriously."

Trevor held up his hands as if being wrongly accused of a crime he did not commit. "Okay. Take it easy. I'm just happy to see a friendly face."

Charlotte smiled. "Me too."

Trevor glanced at the rest of the group standing at a distance behind her. "So these guys are okay? They're not traitors? That's what everyone was saying before this whole thing went down.

"It's okay, they're with me, unless you consider me a traitor."

"As long as you don't stab me in the back, I'm good. I see Vince over there, but where's Saul?"

"He didn't make it out. Simon got to him."

"I'm sorry to hear that." He looked to Vince and nodded his head. "Who's the girl?"

Charlotte turned to Izzy. "You're not going to believe this. She's Greene's daughter."

Trevor flinched, unprepared to hear those words. "Daughter?"

"That's what she says. We found her hiding in Greene's evacuation pod."

Trevor looked stunned. "Holy crap. I didn't know he had a daughter."

"No one did, as far as I know. He's been keeping her hidden."

"Huh, interesting. So, what now? It looks like you've got a nice little village here. Is this a place we can stay? At least until it calms down back in the City."

"We were just about to discuss what to do next. You can listen in if you want."

He looked back at the others that were with him. "I think that would be best. All of these people don't have a home anymore. The Spire is all they know, and now it's gone."

"Come on," Charlotte said. "I'll introduce you to the others." They walked over to the group. "Everyone, this is Trevor Hubble. He's my coworker and good friend. These people worked in the Spire. They have nowhere to go now."

Rupert stuck his hand out. "It's a pleasure to meet you. Any friend of Charlotte's is a friend of ours."

Trevor took his hand firmly and shook. "I want you to know that I worked for Greene, but I have no allegiance to him. It was just a job. I didn't support the decisions he made against you. I think everyone here feels the same way."

"That's good to know," Rupert said.

Alan jumped impatiently. "Now that introductions are out of the way, can we get back to business? What do we plan to do next?"

Rupert nodded. "Let's discuss this inside. It's cold out here. Tell your people they can wait in the cabins. They're all vacant."

Trevor chuckled. "*My* people, huh? I guess I just became their representative." He started walking back. "I'll be there in five minutes."

The group entered the cabin as Trevor went to welcome *his* people to their new home.

NINE

WHEN TREVOR ENTERED the room, the others were standing in a circle, waiting patiently. "So we're standing, huh? No sitters?"

Rupert gestured to a chair. "Please, help yourself."

"Thanks," Trevor said, pulling the chair over. "I've been walking all day. Got to rest my legs for a bit." He sat down and let out a sigh of relief. "I don't get out of The Spire much. I've done more walking today than I've done all month."

Charlotte laughed. "Shut up, Trevor. We all know you're an old fart."

"And proud of it," he said, holding his head up high. "It means people don't ask me to do stuff for them."

"Let's get started," Rupert said. "First, Trevor, you know all of us, correct?"

"That is correct. I think everyone in The Spire knows who you are. All except her." He pointed to Izzy.

She waved her hand over her head and smiled.

Rupert nodded. "I'm afraid that's somewhat of a mystery to all of us. Her name is Izzy. She says she's Victor Greene's daughter. That's all we know."

Trevor rubbed his chin. "Very interesting."

"If you don't mind," Ella said, "could you tell us who you are? What did you do in The Spire?"

"Of course." Trevor crossed his legs. "My name is Trevor Hubble. I am a monitor agent, just like Charlotte. But unlike her glamorous life in the vitality sector, I work in the exciting field of cosmetics." He raised his voice with fake enthusiasm.

Alan nodded. "Cosmetics, huh?"

"Yep! I deal with makeup, mostly. People try on lipstick or eye shadow or whatever, and I write it all down in my journal. It's very unrewarding." This last part he said with a smile.

"Quit complaining," Charlotte said, nudging his shoulder. "You have to work your way up. That's what I did."

"But you were a soldier. That's different. You had training. You can fight and think on your feet. Greene could trust a soldier. I sit in a chair all day and watch people stare in a mirror doing this." He puckered his lips and pretended to put on lipstick.

"You're just impatient. A promotion was coming. Greene respected his workers."

"It sounds like you're defending the man that locked you up."

"I didn't agree with all of his decisions, but he *did* treat us with respect. At least, until I turned against him."

Trevor waved her off. "Yeah, yeah. I've heard this twenty times before. The fact is, the man was a nut." He glanced at Izzy. "No offense, but your dad was a nut. Granted, Simon was a bigger, crazier nut, but they were both still nuts. Simon was a walnut, and Greene was a peanut." A smug smile landed on his face.

Alan laughed. "I like this guy."

Charlotte rolled her eyes. "You're always thinking of food, aren't you Trevor?"

He patted his moderate belly. "What can I say? I'm a man who loves to eat."

"If Greene moved you up to a better sector you would've hated it. You're too laid back. You can't handle the pressure."

"Yeah, I guess you're right. So I'm forever stranded in the land of mascara…Well, not anymore I suppose. Now we're all in the same boat. Banished from The City, stuck in this limbo of a village."

"This is our home," Ella said, slightly irritated.

"And we're not banished," Charlotte said. "We can go back."

Trevor shook his head. "And get lynched by Simon's crew? No, thank you."

"They're all in the Spire right now. We don't have to dock there. We can go to the entrance on the other side. If we change out of our uniforms, no one will ever know we work for Greene."

Trevor pointed to Vince. "People will recognize him for sure. His face has been plastered on every television screen for the past week."

"We would have to be discreet," Vince said, "but I think we could do it."

Alan looked at Vince. "Why do you want to go back?"

"Simon's still in charge. We need to stop him."

Trevor snorted. "There's no way we're getting anywhere close to the Spire. That place is crawling with Crowns."

"That will always be the case," Vince said. "Wherever Simon is, there will be Crowns. That doesn't change the fact that he's a menace who needs to be stopped."

"Well," Alan said, "I guess we know what Vince is voting for."

"I'm not going back," Ella said. "We just got home. There's no reason to go back. The only thing waiting for us there is more pain and misery."

Rupert stepped forward with Fred perched comfortably on his shoulder. "I agree. We should try to move on with our lives. A lot of bad things have happened. We have the City to thank for that. The last thing I want to do is go back. We have a good village here. Let's stay and build up the community we used to have."

"I respect that Snow Peak is your home," Charlotte said, "but it's not mine. I have no reason to stay. For me, home is back in the City. It's Trevor and Izzy's home too."

Trevor shook his head. "There's no way I'm going back. I'll stay out here where I'm a good safe distance from Simon and his psycho followers. I'm sure the rest of my people feel the same way."

"You can't bring Izzy back," Ella said. "She's so much safer here. The minute they find out she's Greene's daughter, her life will always be in danger."

"They don't have to know," Charlotte said. "We can hide it."

"I want to go back," Izzy said quietly.

Ella walked up and knelt by her side. She spoke softly. "Honey, it's not safe for you there."

Tears welled up in the young girl's eyes. "I want to go back home. Please? Can I go back home?"

"She will be safe," Charlotte said with confidence. She wrapped her arms around Izzy and pulled her in close. "I will make sure that she's safe."

Ella shook her head and backed away. "It sounds like you've already made up your minds."

"And it sounds like you have as well," Vince said. "It was a pleasure knowing you for as long as I did. I can truly call you my friends."

"Likewise," Rupert said, sticking out his hand.

Vince took his hand and shook.

Alan watched with eager confusion. "Wait, so that's it? That's the plan? We're just splitting up after everything we've been through?"

"We can't stop them if they want to go back," Rupert said. "All we can do is wish them the best."

Alan's head shifted back and forth between the two parties. "I want to go back too," he blurted out.

"You what?" Ella said with surprise.

"I want to go back to the City with them."

Ella's face held a look of strong concern. "But why? We're home."

Alan shook his head. "Everyone we knew here is dead. My wife. Your mother. Martha. Carl. I have no reason to stay. I don't think I can handle being around this place anymore. Not after seeing the bloodbath yesterday. That image is burned into my head. Every time I step outside, I will see that pile of bodies, stacked up with the dead eyes of the ones I love. Every time I wake up in the morning. Melinda's side of the bed will be cold." He looked down to his feet. "No, I can't stay here. The City may be dangerous, but I won't be haunted by this place."

Silence lingered as they let his words settle. Trevor knew nothing of the *massacre* Alan spoke of, but even he had the sense to keep his mouth shut. Clearly, something terrible had happened, and these people were in mourning.

Finally, Rupert spoke up. "We can't stop them, and we can't stop you, Alan. If you want to go, there's nothing holding you back."

Ella looked up. "Wait, what? You can't just let him leave."

"It sounds like he's put some thought into this. If he wants to go back, that's his decision. I don't like it either, but it's not up to us. This is Alan's decision, and I respect it."

Ella stared at Alan with a mix of emotions cycling through her veins. Should she be angry? Sad? Supportive? She knew deep down that she should be supportive, but it was difficult. They were the three remaining people from Snow Peak. There was no one else. It felt wrong to split up.

Deep down, she knew it was not just the three of them. She had other people as well. Of course she did. They may not be from Snow Peak, but Vince and Charlotte were just as part of the family as Rupert and Alan. But they were leaving too. They were returning to a place of certain danger. Why couldn't they see that Snow Peak was their new home?

These thoughts swam through her head as she stared at Alan. She knew she should say something, but when she opened her mouth, nothing came out. She could not find the words. So instead, she just stood there with tears welling up in her eyes.

Alan walked over and wrapped his arms around her, slowly rocking side to side. "I know," he said softly. "We just got back. The last thing I want to do is split up again, but I can't live here. I can't call this place home anymore."

"But you can call the City your home?" Her voice was soft and broken.

"In time, maybe. It's a huge place. We've only seen a sliver of it. The rest of the City might not be so bad." He loosened his grip and held her at arm's length, looking at her face. "You can come with us. See how it turns out. Home is where your loved ones are, isn't it? So come with us and find our new home."

"We don't need a new home. Rupert and I are here, so why can't this be your home?"

"I already told you. Home is a place where your loved ones are, not a place where you've lost so many. Just come with us."

Ella backed away and shook her head. "No, I can't."

They looked at each other and realized they would not agree. The group would split up, and the Snow Peak community was no more.

Rupert walked over and placed a hand on his shoulder. "Good luck out there. We'll be thinking of you." He looked to Charlotte, Vince, and Izzy. "All of you."

Fred hopped off Rupert's shoulder and onto Alan's. She gently caressed her face against his. A final goodbye. He stroked her tiny head. "I'll miss you too, girl." She fluttered over to Vince and did the same thing.

"I'll miss all of you," Vince said. "It's been a long time since I've felt like part of a community. It was nice. Despite everything that happened to us, I'm glad it was with this group. You make good company. Good friends."

"And who knows?" Alan said. "Maybe we'll come back. Maybe you're right, and the City sucks. And if it doesn't, and we end up staying, we can come back to visit. It's really not *that* far."

Ella sniffled and smiled. "That would be nice."

Alan mirrored her smile, and then looked at Vince and Charlotte. "Shall we?" They both nodded and gathered their bags.

Ella and Rupert walked with them to the edge of the woods, where they hugged and made their final goodbyes. Rupert supplied them with food for the trip. Alan raised his hand and waved. "Don't get too cozy without us." And with that, the four of them turned around and entered the woods, leading back to the snow plains. Back to the cave. Back to the boat. Back to the City.

TEN

TRISH LOOKED OUT at the square, surveying the surrounding area. The place was big and spacious, with lots of room for a stage and large audience. Birds flew across the clear blue sky, and a cool breeze ruffled her hair. She turned to Warren, who was busy posting fliers on the wall. "I like it. This is a good place for the ceremony."

"I told you," Warren said, breaking off a strip of adhesive and sticking it to the wall. "My buddies did a good job. They found this place for dirt cheap."

"How did they manage that?"

"The guy volunteered the square for us to use. He said he liked what we're doing. He believes the ceremony is good for all of us. They tried to offer him at least some money, but he refused. It just goes to show you how much this event means to people. All we need to do is rent the stage and speakers, and we're set."

"Do you really think people will come?"

He nodded. "I'm certain people will come. You've seen all of the people on the streets. They're all from the Spire. A ceremony like this will be important to all of them. They've lost loved ones, their homes, and they've lost Mr. Greene. This ceremony will honor all of those and bring hope for the future." He glanced around the square. "Honestly, I don't know if this place will be big enough."

"Are you kidding me? This place is huge."

"And so is our audience. If all goes well, I hope to fill this entire venue. If this place is too small, that would be the best problem in the world. It means we have more support than I expected, and more people to take back the Spire. That's why we're putting up these fliers. We want as many people to know as possible. Here, help me put them up." He split his pile in half and handed one of them to Trish.

She studied the one on top and read the large text.

REMEMBER THE FALLEN
Join us in honoring the lost souls of friends
and loved ones. There will be a special
dedication to VICTOR GREENE, the man
who helped us all. Hear inspiring words
from speaker TRISH BEAUMONT, who
worked closely with Mr. Greene before his
untimely passing.

She followed Warren's lead, sticking strips of adhesive to the wall. "This will get the word out, but what if Simon sees them? Are you worried he'll try to stop the ceremony?"

"It's something I've thought about, and no, I'm not worried. Similar memorial events have been popping up in other districts. Right now his men are located in the Eastern District. They have no reason to hop over to the west when there are plenty of other places in between doing the same thing."

"What if you're wrong?"

"That's a chance I'm willing to take. This cause is too important to flake out just because we're scared. Fear is never a good reason to give up."

Trish nodded and peered back out at the empty square. "How big is the stage again? Where will we be standing?"

Warren placed the stack of fliers down. "Let me show you." He walked to the center of the square and took a few steps back. "The stage will be here. We're on a tight budget, so it's not the biggest stage ever, but it's good enough." He pointed out to the empty space in front of him. "The rest of this area will be for the crowd. Everyone is welcome. We'll have speakers set up there and there." He pointed to the sides. "And along the front of the stage as well. We want to make sure everyone can hear us."

"You really have this all planned out," Trish said, crossing her arms.

"I've never organized something like this before, but I've seen plenty of Mr. Greene's conferences. I've seen Simon's rallies too. They all have the same setup, so I figured I would copy it. If it works for them, it'll work for us. The only thing I'm missing is the jumbo screen above the stage, but like I said, we're on a tight budget. We were just barely able to afford the speakers." A look of panic hit his face. "Or maybe we should get a jumbo screen. But how in the world am I going to afford it?"

Trish shook her head. "Relax. It'll be fine. We don't need one. Mr. Greene and Simon are all about showmanship. They go over the top with their conferences and rallies. They've been trying to outdo each other for ages. We have no competition. We just want to get our message across. What we have already will do just fine."

Warren sighed with relief. "Good. This whole thing is very stressful. Everything has to go just right. The fate of the City depends on it, after all. With stakes like that, there's no room for error."

"Don't think of it like that. I have no doubt it will be a success. People need a way to grieve, and this is the perfect opportunity. Not much can ruin that."

"You're right," he said, walking back to the fliers. "I'm overthinking it. Everything will go smoothly, I'm sure." He pointed to the wall across the square. "Go put some fliers on that wall. We have enough over here."

ELEVEN

ALAN PEERED AT the City wall, a distant relic that was slowly approaching. They had been gone for no more than two weeks, and now they were back. Vince saw him deep in thought and walked over to join him by his side.

"Do you think she's mad at me?" Alan asked.

"No, she's just confused. We all are. With everything going on, it wears on you. We all handle these situations differently. She wants to keep the group together. That's understandable, respectable even, but we all have different visions of the future. Ours isn't in Snow Peak, it's back in the City."

"She still has Rupert at least."

Vince nodded. "There's no doubt she's mad at me."

"With good reason," Alan said, turning to face him. "I know you were put in a difficult situation. I know Greene is the real one to blame, but everyone we know is gone, and you're the one person who could have stopped it."

"I could have tried, but the odds were unlikely, even if I *did* tell you."

"Yeah," Alan said, looking back to the wall. "You're probably right. It doesn't make it any easier to forgive you, though. I'm doing my best, but Ella is a tough nut to crack. It'll take some time for her."

"Maybe it's good we're splitting up. She needs her space from me, at least for now."

"But not from me," Alan said. "If anything, she needs me even closer now."

"It's not up to her. You couldn't stand being in that place anymore, just like she couldn't stand to leave it. It's unfair to ask each other to go against that instinct."

"It is strange. I surprised myself when I said I wanted to come back with you. There's something about the City. Our time there wasn't peaches and cream, but it wasn't all that bad either. The wonders of technology. The promise of a longer, happier life, with medical breakthroughs we couldn't even imagine."

Vince nodded. "If I had to choose one word to describe the City, it would be potential. For both good and bad."

"I guess we saw a bit of both."

"With Greene gone and Simon on top, who knows where that potential will swing?"

"Simon isn't trying to lead, though. He doesn't want power. He just didn't want Greene to have it."

"That's what he says, but will he change his mind? There's no one to get in his way now. He has an army of followers and everything else he needs to take Greene's position. Only time will tell if he takes advantage of that power. Personally, I don't know what's worse. The City under Simon's rule, or the City with no ruler at all. Either way, things will be different. They'll be complicated."

"And we'll be prepared for anything," Alan said. "We've already endured so much. There's nothing he can throw at us that we can't handle."

"I hope you're right, but I suspect otherwise. With a man that crazy, it's hard to predict anything."

"Hey!" Charlotte shouted from inside. "Izzy's having another seizure! I need your help!"

They ran back inside, where Izzy was convulsing on the bed. This episode seemed more violent than the first. Her spine arched up and down, her arms flailed at her sides, and her head shook at a frightening rate. An unsettling moan rose from her lips in sporadic waves.

Charlotte looked to Alan in a panic. "What do I do?"

"Why are you asking me?" he asked, trotting over to help.

"What did you do last time?"

"I just held her head, I think. I was a little distracted by the boatload of soldiers shooting at us."

Charlotte gently held Izzy's head in place.

Vince walked over and secured her legs. "Just make sure she doesn't fall off the bed. The seizure should pass soon."

"You're right," Alan said. "It only lasted a few minutes last time."

"Is she in any danger?" Charlotte asked. "There's nothing we can do to make it better?"

Alan shook his head. "As long as she doesn't hit her head or fall, that's all we can do. Last time she was completely fine once it was over. I think she's used to having these things."

They watched her body wriggle and squirm. Her eyes rolled back, showing only the whites.

"How could you ever get used to something like this?" Charlotte said to herself. "It looks so painful."

They stood over Izzy and let the seizure reach the end of its cycle. When her body finally came to a rest, her eyes rolled forward, and she lay still, panting.

"Are you okay, honey?" Charlotte asked.

Izzy opened her mouth, and a dribble of blood fell from her lips. "I think I bit my tongue."

"Let me see."

Izzy opened her mouth and stuck out her tongue. There was a small laceration at the tip, where her tooth had sliced through.

"It's just a small cut. Did you hurt anything else?"

She shook her head and smiled.

"What do you call these things?" Alan asked. "They scare the hell out of me every time."

She shrugged. "It's just a seizure. I have them all the time. It's no big deal."

"No big deal?" Alan said. "It looked like a pretty big deal to me."

"Daddy says I have them because I'm special. I'm not like other people."

"What does he mean by that?" Alan said, frustrated.

"You clearly aren't a parent," Charlotte said. "He means that Izzy is the most precious thing in the world to him. He would do anything for her. He would give up anything, even his life."

"And what does that have to do with the seizures?" Alan asked.

Charlotte shrugged. "I don't know, but he was definitely trying to protect her. He kept her hidden from the public for, what, ten years?"

"Regardless," Vince said turning to talk directly to Izzy, "what did your father do when you had these seizures? What should *we* do?"

"Nothing," she answered. "He held my head like you do, but he didn't do anything else. He just waits until they're over."

"Huh," Alan said, dissatisfied. "Really? That's it?"

"They tire me out, but they don't hurt me." She moved her tongue in her mouth. "I don't usually bite my tongue, though."

"Okay," Vince said, decidedly more satisfied than Alan. "So next time, we know what to do. Hold your head and wait."

Izzy and Charlotte nodded in agreement. Alan shrugged. "If you say so."

Charlotte glanced out the window on the far side of the room. She saw the approaching wall. "We're getting close. We should get ready. I have no idea who or what will be waiting for us on the docks. I'm hoping we can sneak in quietly, but we should be prepared, in case we encounter hostiles."

"Hostiles?" Alan said, sarcastically stroking his chin. "Why would anyone be hostile towards us? Oh right, the psycho lunatic that killed Greene and tried to kill us. I forgot about that guy."

They walked outside to see the wall in all of its glory. It was just as large as they remembered. The towering sight of the barrier had not lost its stunning effect.

Alan pointed to the Spire, which poked up in the distance. "The Spire's all the way over there."

"I steered us away from that area," Charlotte said. "It's too dangerous to go directly to the Spire. We don't know what it's like right now. We're entering through a different gate."

"Gate?" Alan asked. "There are gates? That would have been useful the first time around."

"Yes, there are four gates. Three dispersed along the wall and one at the Spire."

"That's the one Barnabus was taking me to," Alan said.

"Correct. Greene had all of his test subjects shipped to the Spire's docks."

"You mean prisoners," Vince said.

"Right, prisoners. Sorry. Force of habit. Anyway, we're not going there." She pointed far to the left, where two large columns stood in place of the wall. "That's where we're going. Between those two pillars is the Western Gate. It's usually operated by Greene's men, but with Greene gone, there's no way to know what we're up against. That's why we need to be careful. For all we know, Simon is posted in there, waiting for us."

"He doesn't know we're coming," Alan said. "And even if he did, he wouldn't know which gate we're at."

Charlotte turned and pointed to the camera mounted above them. "There's a good chance he knows."

"He's been watching us this whole time?" Alan shouted. "Why in the world didn't we disable them?"

"We could have, but it wouldn't matter. There are cameras all over, and this boat has a locator device. If Simon really wanted to, he could find us. But who knows? Maybe he didn't bother looking."

Alan scoffed. "That makes me feel better."

Vince looked at the bag of guns sitting by the bed. "Whatever is waiting for us, Charlotte's right. We need to be ready to protect ourselves. I know we're far from the Spire, but if there are any Crowns in there, there's no doubt they'll try to kill us. Others may want us dead too."

"Like who?" Alan asked.

"A lot of Greene's people think we betrayed him. They think we're working with Simon. You may be okay walking the streets," He pointed to Alan and Charlotte. "They may not recognize you, but like Trevor said, my face was broadcast to the entire City. Everyone knows what I look like. In any case, we should all take precautions and cover our faces anyway."

"Vince is right," Charlotte said, walking to the beds. "We'll cut up these sheets and wear them as scarves. Of course, no one knows about Izzy, so she doesn't need one."

Alan looked at Charlotte, with the sheets in her hands, and to Vince, with guns in his. "So let me get this straight. Our plan is to walk in there and hope that no one recognizes us, and if they do, we charge in, guns blazing."

Vince and Charlotte nodded.

"Okay then," Alan said, shrugging. "Let's do it."

Vince cut long strips from the sheets and Charlotte inspected their guns. Alan wandered to the pantry to stock up on food. They met at the front of the boat, just as it was pulling into the gate. The huge swinging doors were already wide open.

"Hmm," Charlotte said, carefully studying the gate. "They usually keep these closed. Greene didn't much care for outsiders. At least not the ones that weren't test subjects."

"Simon must have opened them," Alan said. "He's all about freedom after all, right? Just like the prisoners in the Spire. Free to stay or free to leave."

"Live free forever," Vince said, recalling the Rodin motto. It was the same motto Harry Hedcrown carried over when he first formed the Crowns.

"Live free forever," Alan repeated. "As long as you agree with Simon. Otherwise, Live free until he shoots you in the head."

The boat slid through the gate and into the docking area. The place was eerily quiet. Dozens of boats were docked against the wooden platforms, none of them occupied. Piles of cargo sat out, unattended. Not a soul was around. The only sound was that of their motor, growling along as they passed by other boats, searching for a vacant spot.

Charlotte steered towards the end of the dock, where there were plenty of spaces. She butted up against the platform and threw the rope around a nearby post. Once they were secure, she wrapped the self-made scarf around her face and hopped out. "I'll check the area. Watch the girl while I'm gone."

She jogged up and down each path, checking the windows of every boat. Vince and Alan stood on the deck, marveling at the size of the place. They knew the City was big, but the sight of so many boats was overwhelming. They were still both new to the technology of the City, motorized boats included.

Charlotte returned with her gun lowered. "The area is clear. We're alone, for now."

"So where to next?" Alan asked.

"Next, we go to the Spire," Vince said. "To find Simon."

"Right," Alan nodded. "How far are we?"

Charlotte considered the question. "Let's see. The Western Gate is the closest one to the Spire, other than the Spire gate of course. It's about five miles away.

"Five miles?" Alan said shrugging. "I guess we walked in the snow plains for five days. What's another five miles?"

"It is a long distance to go unseen," Vince said. "Especially in a place this densely populated."

Charlotte nodded. "So we stick to the shadows and move quickly. Stay away from the main streets. The tunnels are completely off limits. Everything underground is Crowns territory."

"Isn't everything Crown territory now?" Alan said.

She shrugged. "I guess, but it will be far worse underground. We have no reason to go down there anyway."

"We need to look out for cameras too," Vince added.

"That will be difficult," Charlotte said. "Greene's cameras are on almost every block."

"We did it when we were with Simon. Otherwise, Greene would have seen us coming."

Charlotte looked up at the camera mounted on their boat. "Maybe we don't have to worry about them. That camera up there was staring us in the face for the whole trip, and there's no one here waiting for us. If he was paying attention to the cameras, he would have sent someone. Maybe he missed Greene's camera systems, or he just lost interest."

"Okay," Vince said. "So we won't worry about the cameras, but keep an eye out for people and stay hidden if you see anyone. There's no way to tell if they're friendly or not, but we can't afford to risk it. If anyone recognizes us, if they blow our cover, our trip suddenly becomes ten times as dangerous. Does everyone understand?"

They nodded.

Vince wrapped the scarf around his face and pulled his hood up. "Good, then let's go."

TWELVE

V INCE, CHARLOTTE, AND Alan briskly walked along the side of the road. Izzy sat upon Charlotte's shoulders.

"You know the way, right?" Alan asked. He felt the need to whisper even though no one was in sight.

"Maybe," Charlotte said.

"Maybe? You're telling me we don't know where we're going?"

"We know the general direction. That should be enough."

"Why in the world don't you know the way? This is your home, isn't it?"

"The Spire is my home. It *was* my home. The day I went on that mission with you was the first time I left the

Spire in fifty years, maybe more. I've studied maps, but the City is massive. I only know the major roads. You know, the ones we're trying to avoid."

Alan threw his arms up. "Well, I've lost all hope. We're going to get lost in this maze and end up on the opposite side of the City. Then again, that might not be such a bad thing. As far as I'm concerned, the further away from that thing, the better."

Vince shook his head. "We must go back. Someone has to stop Simon. He's too unpredictable to have such power."

Alan dismissively waved his hand. "Yeah, yeah. Don't worry. I was just joking. I'm looking forward to seeing the old labs. Ah, the memories."

Voices came from around the corner, two people in deep conversation. The four of them dashed to the nearest wall and pressed their bodies flat against the cold concrete, hidden in shadow.

The two strangers stopped in the middle of the intersection, chatting away.

"What do you think those signs mean?" said the voice of a man.

A woman answered. "You mean the wanted signs?"

"Yeah, it doesn't make sense. Why would a girl so young have a bounty on her head?"

"She's important to someone. Or at least Simon seems to think so."

"Simon is a weird guy. Do you think it's for, you know…"

"No. He's a crazy son of a bitch, but he's not like that. Knowing him, he'll probably hand her a gun and tell her to shoot some poor labbie."

"You think there are still some around? Labbies I mean."

"I'm sure of it. He must be holding them captive."

"Why wouldn't he just kill them?" the man asked.

"If he kills them, he loses his leverage. His power."

"Leverage for what? Greene's dead. He's already won."

"I don't know," the woman answered. "Maybe he knows someone's coming."

"Or maybe he's just a sick bastard."

"That is also very likely." She paused for a moment. "You know what, you're probably right. Why does he ever do anything? Because he's one sick bastard."

"I can get on board with that."

"Oh, we're late."

"Let's get going then. Don't want to miss the ceremony. It's important. We need to honor the ones we've lost.

"Do you know where we're going?"

"Yeah, this way."

The strangers moved down the street, away from the four of them pressed against the wall. "What was that about?" Alan asked.

"Wanted posters of a girl?" Charlotte said. "Could it be Izzy? Could he somehow know Greene's secret?"

Vince looked up at another camera, staring at them from up high. "You said there are cameras everywhere. He must have seen her on the monitors."

"Even if that's true, the cameras don't have microphones. The only way he could hear us is through a portable microphone. There's no way he knows she's his daughter. To him, she's just a random girl who decided to tag along."

"Well he wants her for some reason," Alan said. "Where do you think those two are going? They mentioned a ceremony?"

"They said it was to honor the ones they've lost," Vince said.

"We should go," Charlotte said.

Vince and Alan both glanced at her as if they had misheard what she said.

"Are you crazy?" Alan asked. "I thought we were trying to *avoid* people. That ceremony is guaranteed to be swarming with people. People who think we're traitors.

As far as they know, we're the reason all of those people are dead in the first place."

"Which is true, I suppose," Vince added. "My plan was to rescue you and take down Greene, but I put other people's lives in danger without realizing it."

"They were going to break through anyway," Charlotte said. "Your arrival may have sped up the process, but Simon was determined, and Greene wasn't equipped to handle his methods. They broke through the first wall before your group even showed up."

"That won't make any difference to these people," Alan said. "Directly or indirectly, those people died because of us. It's a slap in the face to show up to their funeral."

"Remember," Charlotte said, "the Spire was my home. I knew a lot of people who died that day. Some of them were close friends. I know the ceremony will be crowded. I know there will be some risk, but it's very small. We can stay in the back and keep our faces covered. I promise, no one will recognize us." She sighed. "You got your chance to mourn, now it's my turn."

Alan glanced down at his feet. "Damn it! When you put it like that, now I feel bad. I guess we're going to the ceremony."

Vince nodded. "We don't stay long, we don't talk to anyone, and we don't show our faces. If it is Izzy's face on these wanted posters, we will need to cover her face as well."

"Here," Charlotte said, pulling out a spare cloth. She gently wrapped it around Izzy's face. "Is that comfortable?"

Izzy nodded. "Yup," she said in a muffled voice.

"Good. Come on. We'll follow them, but let's keep our distance."

Alan peered down at the two people down the street, walking away as they turned the corner. "We' don't want to lose them either. Hurry up."

They jogged to the corner and peeked their heads around. The man and woman were halfway up the block. They waited a bit longer and swung around the bend, walking casually down the street and keeping a close eye on their two guides.

Vince pointed to a wall on their right. "Look," he said. The others turned to see a wall littered with posters. "There's the wanted poster."

Charlotte trotted over and grabbed a copy. She ran back, holding it up to examine. "Well, this is definitely Izzy."

Alan leaned over to see. "I don't get it. Why would Simon want Izzy?"

"Maybe he knows something we don't," Vince said.

"Like what? We're the ones that know she's Greene's daughter. I thought we were the ones with the secret."

Vince shrugged. "I don't know, but he knows something."

"I don't like it," Alan said. "This whole thing makes me uncomfortable."

"No one said coming back would be easy," Charlotte said. "But *someone* has to stop Simon."

Vince shook his head. "Simon said he would give up his power once Greene was gone. I'm beginning to think that won't happen."

"Of course it won't," Alan said. "A nut like that can't resist power, even if he thinks he can. I didn't believe it for a second when those words left his mouth."

"I had my doubts, but some of the things he said before the attack, he almost sounded sane."

Alan laughed. "There is no way that man is sane. Not in the slightest. A sane man doesn't use children as weapons or sacrifice thousands of people just to send a message. A sane man would not shoot his own troops for absolutely no reason at all. I've said it a hundred times, but that guy is nuts. He has anger issues. He throws tantrums, and if you get in his way, he shoots you. We all saw it. Saul didn't have to die like that."

"Enough," Vince said. "We don't need to dwell on the past. What's done is done. Focus on the task at hand."

"All I'm saying is, if a man like that is put in a place of power, he will *never* give it up."

"And that's why we have to take it from him," Vince said. His face, stone cold.

THIRTEEN

A S THEY FOLLOWED the man and woman down the street, another group of three turned onto the road. They were also talking about the ceremony. Vince and the others stopped their conversation, anxiously walking beside these new strangers. More people joined, and they soon found themselves stuck in the center of a small crowd, heading towards the ceremony. Vince kept his head down, hoping no one would recognize them.

The strangers paid no attention to them, but they remained silent anyway, too nervous to say a word. Charlotte finally looked to her side and whispered, "I think we're okay. They don't recognize us."

"Don't take any chances," Vince whispered back.

"This was a mistake," Alan said. "We should have stuck to the plan and headed straight for the Spire."

Vince kept his eyes forward and his head down. "Too late now. We're surrounded. There's no way to get out without drawing attention. All we can do now is follow them and hope for the best."

"Shoot," Alan said. "I hate hope-for-the-best. It never works out."

"Hey, we're still alive," Charlotte said. "That has to count for something. We'll be okay as long as we don't make a scene."

Izzy pressed up against Charlotte, trembling as the crowd grew denser. Charlotte wrapped an arm around her shoulder and pulled her in closer.

The movement of the crowd slowed to a stop, and they found themselves in front of a modest stage. Vibrant flowers were stacked at the center, with pictures of faces scattered around. Hanging from the front of the stage was a sign that read, *Never Forget*. People from the crowd threw paper on stage. Pictures of loved ones, and letters of grief.

"When does it start?" Alan asked to no one in particular.

A lady to his right turned around. "Any minute now. It's so nice that they're doing this. A ceremony like this means so much." She held up a picture to show Alan.

"This is my son. He was working in the Spire during the attack. He didn't make it out."

"I'm sorry to hear that," Alan said. "It was truly a horrible day for all of us. I'm sure your son was a good man." The lady crumpled the paper, pressed it against her lips with loving care, and tossed it onto the stage.

"Thank you for saying so. If you don't mind me asking, who did you lose?"

Alan thought about the question for a moment. "My wife, Melinda."

"Do you have a picture of her? You can throw it on stage."

Alan lowered his head. "Sadly I do not. She was a beautiful woman, though."

"Did she work in the Spire?"

"No. She just got caught up in something she wasn't a part of."

"That's a shame."

"She was the nicest woman in the world. Wouldn't hurt a fly. She always put others ahead of herself. She didn't deserve such a cruel death."

"She sounds like a nice person. Perhaps she and my son will meet in the afterlife."

"Yes, perhaps."

A man walked up on stage holding a microphone. "Ladies and gentlemen. If I could have your attention, I would like to begin this ceremony." He waited for the chatter to die down. "Thank you. As you all know, we are here to honor lost friends and family who were taken during the fall of the Spire. It only happened weeks ago, but it feels like ages that we've had to suffer without our loved ones. I know it's difficult, but we will overcome this time of sorrow. Every single one of us has one thing in common. We have lost someone close. We will not let this break our spirits. Instead, we will support each other and grow as a community."

The crowd cheered.

"I think it would be appropriate to take a moment of silence, in respect for those we've lost. Please join me." He lowered his head and closed his eyes. The rest of the crowd did the same.

Vince, Izzy, Charlotte, and Alan closed their eyes as well.

Alan thought of Melinda. Her beautiful eyes. Her laugh. Her smile. Everything she did filled his heart with joy, but she was no longer around, and a black void filled that spot instead. The void was impossible to fill. It would remain there forever.

Charlotte thought of her friends and coworkers. It was the only community she had, and now many of them were gone. A few had made it out, like Trevor, but she would never forget the others. They were all good people. None of them deserved to die.

Izzy thought of her father. The others called him Greene, but to her he was Daddy. He was the only person she knew, other than the labbies, and he was certainly the only person she loved. The one person in her life was taken, the only home she knew was left behind, and now she wandered with strangers, amidst a crowd of people. There were so many faces, but the only one she wanted to see was gone forever.

Vince thought of Saul. Who else was there to think of? Their loss in Snow Peak was tragic, but Saul was his best friend. He was more than that. They defied death for two hundred years, and now for Saul, it was all over. A life spanning two centuries was turned to dust with the pull of a trigger. Behind that trigger stood a mad-man, the one responsible for all of it. Simon, the psycho, as Alan would put it. Vince's memory of Saul was stained by the image of his headless body lying at the feet of that monster.

They had all lost someone close. Death had risen up and snatched their loved ones from the mortal plane, dragging them into the mysterious depths of the afterlife. And what the afterlife brought, no one knew. None would know until death returned to claim their own lives. All they could do was show respect, and pray that life after death led to happiness.

"Thank you," the man continued, breaking the silence. "Now I would like to introduce our special guest. She is one of Mr. Greene's former employees. She spent her days in the labs, working with subjects and helping to improve the City. Her name is Trish Beaumont."

A young woman joined the man on stage. He handed the microphone over and stepped back. The woman wore the familiar white lab coat. A pair of thick-framed glasses sat on the top of her nose.

"Thank you, Warren," she said, with her voice projecting through the speakers. "As he said, my name is Trish. I used to work in the Spire. I was there during the attack. There were a lot of brave men and women defending their home. Defending what made this City so great. Victor Greene was a triumphant man."

"I guess this is a ceremony for Greene," Alan whispered.

"Of course they're going to mention him," Charlotte said. "He's one of the fallen, and had such a big impact on these people."

"He was a man with a vision," the woman on stage continued, adjusting her glasses every few minutes. "A man whose only wish was to help others. We were all touched by his kindness. His generosity was boundless."

She paused and lowered her head. "In the last couple of years, I worked very close with Mr. Greene. I saw him every day. I worked by his side on a project close to his heart. Sadly, in his absence, the project will never come to light. Too much was lost in the wreckage. But that doesn't mean we will forget what he did for us. He sacrificed so much to make our lives better. It is not only our duty to carry on his work. It is our privilege. It's not what he would have wanted, but what he would have expected."

The crowd broke out in hollers and cheers, clapping and stomping their feet. Looking around, it became apparent to both Vince and Alan, that these were true supporters of the man they were trying to kill.

The woman waved to the crowd and handed the microphone back to the man. "Inspiring words, Trish. An appropriate way to start off this ceremony. With a vision of hope for the future. It is true, we will carry on Victor Greene's work. His body has perished, but his name lives on. We will not let Simon scare us with acts of terror. We will come together and strengthen as a community. Simon thinks we'll just give up, but he's wrong. We will not quit. We will persevere—"

A blast shook the ground and bodies flew up in the air. The crowd scattered in fear. They screamed with terror and cried for help, shuffling to escape the area, but they were too tightly packed. Another blast went off, this time from behind. Vince turned away as a mist of blood moved past them. The taste of warm iron filled his mouth and lungs.

There was no room to move, but the crowd pushed anyway. A great force pushed Vince forward and slammed his chest into the person in front of him. The increasing pressure cut off the circulation to his fingers. Alan stood by his side, screaming with discomfort.

Charlotte grabbed Izzy and held her over her shoulders, above the crowd. Izzy's scarf hooked one of Charlotte's buttons and pulled right off. Charlotte ignored it and placed the girl on her shoulders. Some people nearby showed a glimpse of recognition when they saw her face, but most were too panicked to pay attention.

"How do we get out?" Alan yelled to Vince.

As the words left his mouth, two more blasts hit. They were closer and louder than the others. All sounds were muffled by an incessant ringing in their ears. A pocket of dead bodies fell inward to the ground and with the force of the pushing crowd, Vince, Alan, and Charlotte toppled over. Alan guided his fall to catch Izzy from Charlotte's shoulders. A soft bed of corpses broke their fall and more were thrown on top. They were trapped in a sandwich of flesh and blood. Izzy screamed and cried. Tears and drool mixed together, dripping from her chin.

Vince saw the pain in her eyes. He took a deep breath and pushed against the people on top of him. His face turned red, and his veins bulged out as he expended his energy. He lifted three bodies and tossed them aside. He got to his feet and wobbled left and right, dizzy from overexerting himself. After a brief moment of rest, he ran over to Alan, who had caught Izzy in his arms. He pulled bodies off one by one until he could reach Izzy. He pulled her out of the pile.

"Are you okay?" he asked, forgetting about the ringing in his ears. The words came out garbled and nonsensical. He searched her body for cuts and bruises and placed her on the ground to help the others.

Once Alan and Charlotte were up, he glanced around at the chaos. The crowd was scattered with people running in every direction. Limbs littered the ground, and thick blood stained their boots. Amidst the confusion, he saw a woman run into a crowd, strapped with explosives.

"Suicide bombers!" Alan yelled. "That sick bastard. This is a funeral. Does he have no respect?"

"Of course not!" Charlotte yelled back. "Haven't you learned anything about him?"

"But nobody's this cruel." Alan's tone was of disbelief.

"You would usually be right, but Simon is the exception."

"We need to get out of here!" Vince yelled, with the ringing in his ears finally dying down. "Fast!"

Charlotte frantically looked around. "Follow me!" She led them away from the stage towards the back.

A clear path opened up to a street. They sprinted towards the opening, Charlotte holding Izzy in her arms. Bombs exploded on either side of them. Screams echoed, and blood splashed onto the path.

Alan slipped on a fresh patch of blood and fell hard, landing on his back and knocking the wind out of him. He gasped for air, but his lungs would not work.

Vince stopped to help him up. He stuck out his hand and pulled him to his feet. "Are you okay?"

Alan clenched his chest, finally able to breathe. "Yeah I'm good."

Vince nodded, and turned forward to continue, but the gap in the crowd was gone. There was no more path the follow. Instead, four large Crowns were blocking their way. Vince turned in the other direction to see four more.

"You ain't going nowhere," the biggest of the bunch said. They starting closing in, forcing Vince and the others to group together. "Nice scarves you got there." He pointed to Izzy. "It looks like you're missing yours. What a shame." He yanked the scarf from Vince's face. "Oh look who it is. The infamous Vincent Vigo. I would really enjoy killing you. You're lucky he wants you alive." He charged in and punched Vince right in the nose. Vince's eyes rolled back as he fell unconscious.

FOURTEEN

E LLA WAS BLINDED by the glaring light that was hanging from the ceiling. It swung back and forth in a rhythmic pattern. The screech of a chain pierced her ears with each swing. She tried to shade her eyes, but her arms were stuck. She turned her head to see a group of guards holding her wrists to the table she lay on. They were all dressed from head to toe in combat gear. A thick vest, rough gloves, and shiny helmet. She opened her mouth to yell, but nothing came out.

A large figure, the silhouette of a man, hovered over her head, blocking the light. His face was hidden behind a surgical mask. His breath was loud and in sync with the swinging chain.

He held up a scalpel, its metal edge glistening in the artificial light. "Don't worry young girl." His voice was deep and muffled. "You won't feel a thing. You're fast asleep."

Ella tried to tell him that she was not asleep, but still, her voice would not work. She heard her heart thumping in her chest, again, to the rhythm of the chain. As the man's hand moved closer, she saw the sharp edges of the blade. She pulled and pushed her arms, struggling to break free, but the grip on her wrists was too tight. The scalpel plunged below her vision, towards her stomach. She shut her eyes, anticipating the feel of cold metal on her bare skin, waiting for the blade to slice through her belly like butter.

She waited, but nothing came. She opened her eyes to see the man was gone. The rhythmic screech of the chain had stopped, and the swinging light had disappeared. Her arms were free from restraint. There were no more guards in the room. No one in the room at all. Just her. She sat up and looked around.

The room was empty and well-lit with ceiling and floor lights. There was only the table she sat on and a desk in the far corner. A mug sat at the center of the desk. She hopped off the table, touching her bare feet to the cold tile, and walked to the desk. The mug held a steaming liquid. She leaned in and inhaled the scent of fresh tea.

A thump came from across the room. She twisted around, waiting to see if it would happen again. Thump. It came from behind the door in the opposite corner. It was a sliding door, like the ones from the Spire. She approached it with caution, keeping an eye on the flashing button to the left. Thump. Thump. It was the sound of someone pounding on the metal from the other side.

She opened her mouth and found that she was now able to speak. "Hello? Who's there?" She crept even closer and pressed her palm against the door.

Thump. Thump. Thump.

She moved to the left and pressed the flashing button. Nothing happened. She pressed it again, and this time held it down. Still nothing. She pressed it a few more time, and gave up, stepping back to examine the door from a distance.

The thumping grew louder and more rapid. The distressed sound of clawing joined in. She watched the door, both confused and scared of whatever was on the other side. Why did they so desperately want to get in? Thump. Thump. Thump. The rapid frequency reached an intense peak and then fell silent.

She tilted her head, hesitant to do anything at all. She lifted her foot and stepped forward.

The door slid open, and a body shot out towards her, slamming her in the face.

Ella sprung out of her bed in a cold sweat. Her breath was short, and her head was spinning. She was not in the Spire. There were no soldiers. No man with a surgical mask. No thumping. She was safe and sound in her own cabin, stowed away from any danger. An unpleasant feeling dropped to her stomach. She sensed that Vince, Alan, and Charlotte were in great peril. Something had gone horribly wrong.

FIFTEEN

VINCE'S EYES SPRUNG open at the sound of a loud clang. He jolted up in confusion, disoriented by the blinding light through the bars. His eyes adjusted as another loud clang echoed off the walls. He sat up and turned towards the cell next to his. "That won't do any good, Alan. Those bars are thick."

"What else am I going to do?" Alan asked, leaning back and slamming his heel into the steel bars."

"You're wasting your energy."

Alan ignored him and continued to kick. "I can't believe we're back in Greene's goddamn cell room."

"It's Simon's cell room now," Charlotte said from the cell over. "I don't know why he's keeping us here, though. Why didn't he just kill us?"

"Because that's the kind of sicko he is," Alan said, finally giving up on the bars and falling back to lean against the concrete wall. "He enjoys watching us squirm."

"He knows we're here to kill him," Vince said. "Is he really that confident?"

"That's what taking down an empire does to you. It explodes your ego."

"Where's the girl?" Vince asked. "Is she okay?"

"She's not in here with us," Charlotte answered. "And if she is, she's not responding." She cleared her throat. "Izzy! Are you there?"

They waited, but there was no response.

"They must have taken her," Vince said.

"But why take her and leave us?"

Alan sighed. "I don't suppose we're going to make sense of this anytime soon. Can we just focus on getting out of here? Then we can go searching for the girl."

"Right," Charlotte agreed.

"Check your pockets," Vince said. "They must have searched us, but maybe they missed something."

They patted down their clothes. "Nope," Alan said. "I got nothing."

"Me too," Charlotte said.

Vince patted down as well. His fingers ran around his belt. There was nothing there. He felt pants pockets. Also nothing. He felt through his cloak. There was something in his side pocket. "Wait a minute," he said, holding it up between his thumb and index finger. It was a small capsule. "It's the poison capsule."

"From the stealth mission?" Alan asked.

"Yes."

"Why are you carrying that around?"

"I forgot I had it. I don't suppose it will help us get out of these cells." He slipped it back into his pocket. "You were locked in here before. Did you learn anything about these cells?"

"Not really," Alan said. "We didn't have to. You came to the rescue with Humphrey."

Vince glanced at the railing where Humphrey had tumbled over. "Humphrey can't rescue us this time."

Charlotte pointed to the kiosk across the catwalk. "We can use those stations to call Greene's workers. That doesn't do us any good now, though."

"Do they still work?" Vince asked.

"Why does it matter?" Alan said. "It's not like we can reach it, and even if we could, there's no one to call."

"I'm just gathering all of the information we have. You never know what will be useful."

"It should still be functional as long as the power is still on," Charlotte said, "which seems to be the case. Otherwise, they wouldn't have been able to lock us..."

She trailed off and moved closer to the bars to see the kiosk. She pointed to the bottom panel. "That's strange. That light should be on." She looked down to examine the lock on the door. She wiggled the latch with her hand. It was suspiciously loose. She backed away, leaned against the wall for balance, and kicked her weight into the latch. The door popped open. "I'm out."

Alan glanced at her as she walked by. "How in the world did you do that?"

She approached the kiosk and tapped the screen. Nothing happened. "The power is off. At least on this level. The locks don't work properly when the power is off. Simon must have shut it off when he freed everyone, and never bothered to turn it back on."

Vince kicked the latch, and his door swung open as well. Alan looked at him, both surprised and annoyed. "That's what I was doing, and you told me to stop."

"You must have been kicking too softly," Vince said blandly.

"Hey, I take offense to that. I can kick just as hard as either of you."

"You were kicking in the wrong spot," Charlotte said. She tapped her finger against the metal latch. "This is the weak spot."

Alan assumed his kicking stance and slammed his boot into the latch. The door swung open just like the others. "See," he said with a goofy smile. "I kick just as hard."

"Don't hurt yourself," Vince said.

Alan's eyes widened. "Woah, is that sarcasm coming from Vince?" He patted his back. "Would you look at that. He's coming out of his shell."

Vince did not respond.

"So Simon just forgot to lock us in," Alan exclaimed. "We are damn lucky."

"Let's hope that luck keeps up," Charlotte said. "Now that we're out, we need to find Izzy. Our best bet is the top floor, in Greene's office. He's probably up there, and if not, we can use Greene's system to pinpoint recent activity in the Spire."

Alan clapped his hands. "Let's go!" He took a step and hit his foot on the railing. "Ow! It's so dark down here. You don't have one of those portable glowing light doodads, do you?"

Charlotte shook her head. "They took mine away when Greene locked me up."

They took a few deliberate steps, carefully watching their feet. Their bags sat in the cell next to Charlotte's. Alan trotted over to find his. "Wow, he really didn't try to hide our stuff. It's all just lying right here."

"He's getting sloppy," Charlotte said. "I expected him to be smarter than this. These are silly mistakes. Things that a rookie would do."

Alan strapped his bag over his shoulder. "Hey, I'm not complaining. It just makes things easier for us." He pulled out his rifle and examined its condition. "He even left our guns. How considerate."

They gathered their things and headed for the stairs, wading through the darkness of the lower cells. As they ascended the stairs, towards the glass ceiling, the sunlight grew brighter. They passed by numerous empty cells.

"It's crazy," Alan said. "Every single one of these was full just a few weeks ago. Now they're completely abandoned."

Vince studied the cells. Some were stained with urine. "They were not well taken care of down here."

"I knew it was bad," Charlotte said, "but not this bad. I had never seen the cells myself. I just heard rumors."

"Where do you think they all went?" Vince asked. "The prisoners, I mean."

"Into the streets," Alan answered. "Where else would they go?"

"I know," Vince said, "but where on the streets? They don't have homes, do they?"

"Some do," Charlotte said. "The newer prisoners likely have families, but the rest of them have been locked up for most of their life. I doubt they'll survive on the streets. They have no money. No shelter. No one to look after them. They've been dependent on Greene for so long. They probably can't take care of themselves anymore."

They reached the upper levels. Sunlight poured down the center shaft of the room.

"That's a side effect Simon didn't consider," Alan said. "He was all gung-ho for freedom, but some people can't survive in a free world."

"He claims to fight for freedom," Charlotte said, "but didn't much care for the freedom of the people who worked here. Many of them weren't strong supporters of Greene. They were just doing their job. Supporting their families."

"We've said it before," Vince said. "Simon has a twisted sense of justice. That's why we have to stop him."

They reached as high as the stair would go. Level 149.

"There's a separate staircase to the top," Charlotte said. "Or we can take the elevator if it's working." They stood by the familiar security door that kept unauthorized people from getting in and out of the cell room. It was wide open. "It looks like Simon left this door open too."

They left the cell room and entered the maze of hallways. Charlotte knew every twist and turn. Vince and Alan followed her lead. Along the way they encountered three guards, each patrolling a long sweep of the labs. They stayed low, waiting for the right opportunity, and snuck by. She led them out of the restricted zone, and back to the main corridor.

As they walked towards the elevators, they witnessed the wreckage from the day of the attack. Flickering lights. Gun Powder. Debris. Bloodied walls. The incessant buzz of flies congregating around the decaying bodies and the putrid smell. The pungent stench made Alan gag.

"Are you okay?" Vince asked, his eyes watering from the harsh air.

"Yeah, I'll be fine. Someone should really clean this up."

"Who?" Charlotte asked. "Simon's certainly not going to do it."

Alan shrugged. He did not have an answer to the question. He just wanted someone to blame for the wretched smell.

They continued down the hall, holding their scarves over their mouths. It made little difference, but it was better than nothing. They walked past their room, where they had slept for several weeks. Aside from the corpse by the doorway, the room remained largely untouched.

"Man," Alan said. "Those beds were comfortable, but I don't think I could have stood one more night in this place. Everything was so clean. It was *too* clean."

"It's not anymore," Vince said.

They moved on and came to the briefing room. Alan wandered inside. "Ah, more great memories of Greene telling us what to do. Good times."

Charlotte poked her head through the doorway. "Enough messing around," she said. "We need to find Izzy. We can't afford to waste any more time."

"Oh right. Sorry." Alan popped out, and they continued towards the elevators.

They stepped through the sliding doors and Charlotte pressed *150*. "I'm surprised there are so few Crowns here. I expected more."

"The Spire is big," Vince said. "Maybe he has them gathered in a different area."

Charlotte stared up at the display above the door, waiting for the 149 to change to 150. "If he has them gathered anywhere, it's probably in Greene's office."

Alan held up his rifle. "They won't withstand our little trio of misfits."

"We can't go in shooting," Vince said. "We stand no chance."

"We did it before," Alan said. "We'll do it again."

"That was different," Charlotte said. "It was in the middle of chaos. There were distractions, and we had more numbers. The evacuation pods were working too."

"And we didn't all get out alive," Vince added, reminding them of Saul.

"Right," Charlotte said. "If we want to get out alive, we need to have a more thoughtful approach."

"Stealth mission?" Alan asked. A hint of excitement rose up in his voice.

She nodded and grinned. "Stealth mission."

"What's the plan?" Vince asked.

"Well, it's not much of a plan. We just need to make a quiet entrance. Sneak in unnoticed. At least get in far enough to see what we're dealing with. We need to locate Izzy and Simon and figure out how many guards he has. Once we know all of that, we can decide what to do next."

Alan nodded. "Sounds like a plan, man."

The elevator doors slid open, and they tiptoed out. Charlotte held a finger to her lips. "No more talking, and if you must, whisper."

The hallway was in a similar condition to the floor below. Bloodied walls, flickering lights, and littered with bodies. The smell was just as bad too. Vince had a hard time believing that Simon would stay in a place so revolting. He was beginning to suspect that Simon was not in the Spire at all. But Izzy was, and they needed to find her.

They turned the corner and crept along the walls, hidden in shadow and only occasionally illuminated by flickering lights. They heard no one. Saw no one. Just the remnants of the security door at the end of the hall, with metal ends bent back and charred with explosive dust. Lights past the door were off. It was too dark to see inside.

They carefully stepped over bodies, guns raised. They crossed the threshold and pushed through the double doors, into Greene's office. It was pitch black and impossible to see anything. There was only the small flickering ray of light coming in from the hallway.

Charlotte inched over to a switch on the wall "Get ready," she whispered. "I'm switching on the lights."

Vince and Alan both tightened the grip on their guns. She flipped the switch and light poured into the room, blinding all three of them. They dropped their weapons to cover their eyes, but swiped them back up when they remembered the potentially fatal threat in the room. Their eyes adjusted and they got a clear view of the room. It was completely empty. Not a single person in sight. They lowered their weapons and relaxed.

"He's not up here," Alan said. "So much build up for nothing."

"It's good he's not up here," Charlotte said, walking over to the panel. "Now we have control of Greene's system. We can use it to find Izzy. We can control other things too, like the power."

"That's good," Vince said, watching the screen as she logged in.

Alan sauntered about the room, examining the walls and desks. He dug through a pile of papers and found a book, similar to Charlotte's journal. He ran his fingers over the embroidered letters on the cover. *Monitor Journal: Project Monika.* He grabbed it and held it up. "What's this?"

Charlotte pulled her eyes from the screen and glanced at the book. "It looks like a monitor journal."

"Well, I know that. It says that right on the cover. But what's Project Monika?"

Charlotte searched her memory and shrugged. "I don't recall a Project Monika." She squinted and walked over. "Why would a monitor journal be up here in Greene's office? Monitor agents weren't allowed in here."

"Greene's not around anymore," Vince said. "Someone else brought it up after the attack."

"But why?" Alan asked.

Charlotte opened the cover. "It must be important." She flipped through the pages and started reading. Vince and Alan watched her expression transform from curiosity to intrigue. She stopped reading and looked up. "You have to read this."

They gathered together and hovered over the journal, reading Project Monika.

SIXTEEN

PROJECT MONIKA

Monitor Agent: Victor Greene

Day 0   Weight: 1 pound   Length: 1 inch

I have transferred this experiment from Project Nyssa. What started as yet another effort to extend the human lifespan, has turned into something much bigger. Normally I would assign a monitor agent to record these logs, but I want to keep this project small and out of sight. At least for now. Only me and a select few will work on this. I have chosen a team of two labbies. Trish Beaumont and Humphrey Jacks. If necessary, I will request additional help, but I think two will be enough.

A development in the lab today has turned this project into perhaps one of the most important projects in the vitality sector. Potentially in all of the Spire. The results are currently uncertain, but I believe we have created life. Using various samples of my own tissue, we have created a specimen that appears to be growing and exhibits signs of life. It stands at approximately one inch in length and is growing at a surprising rate. We detect a steady heart beat and minimal brain activity. We are storing the specimen in a small glass chamber, submerged in nutrient-rich fluids. We hope this will promote growth. We will continue to monitor all developments closely. I am excited about the potential for this project, but until it yields more stable results, I will continue to keep it hidden from both the public and the rest of my employees.

Day 12　　　Weight: 2 pounds　　　Length: 4 inches
The specimen continues to grow. It now measures four inches in length. Its heart rate remains steady, and its brain activity has increased. Arms and legs have started to form, and I think I see a small pair of eyes. The nutrients from the fluids seem to be working. The specimen remains healthy.

Day 30   Weight: 6 pounds   Length: 10 inches
The specimen is developing quite well. It resembles the shape of a human baby, though it is still very small. I am surprised with how fast the body is maturing. We have moved it to a larger chamber to accommodate for future growth. After close analysis, we have determined that it is a girl. Very exciting and quite surprising! I did not expect a female specimen. I don't even know how it's possible. Perhaps I should name her. Given the name of the project, I suppose I could name her Monika, although that seems too easy. Maybe Laura.

Day 31   Weight: 6 pounds   Length: 10 inches
Not Laura. Isabella.

Day 53   Weight: 13 pounds   Length: 22 inches
Isabella has developed enough to survive outside of her chamber. She no longer needs the fluids to sustain herself. We will continue to care for her as we would a normal child.

Day 54   Weight: 13 pounds   Length: 22 inches
I held her for the first time today. The labbies say she is finally healthy enough to have outside contact, so I asked them to bring her to my office. She looked up at me with her adorable eyes and swung her little arms around. Her

laugh is the most precious laugh I've ever heard. I think I'm ready to share her with the rest of The City. It is a big moment. I'm curious to see how people will react. The creation of life right here in our labs. It could mean big things for the future. I will make the announcement tomorrow.

Day 55   Weight: 13 pounds   Length: 22 inches
Today a group of workers were killed by the Crowns in a terrorist attack. It was a suicide bomber. Simon immediately took responsibility, although I never doubt it was him in the first place. He's a monster. In light of the tragedy, I have canceled my plans to introduce Isabella. After the incident this morning, I question if I ever will. Simon says our experiments are unnatural. He preaches that we shouldn't mess with biology, but my experiments have helped people in so many ways. I've made people happier. We are healthier and live longer, all because of the work we do in these labs. He will never appreciate that. If I reveal Isabella's existence, she will surely become a target.

Day 77   Weight: 17 pounds   Length: 26 inches
There was a bit of a scare today. This morning Isabella had a violent seizure. It lasted approximately thirty seconds. It was the longest thirty seconds of my life.

Fortunately, we handled the situation in a timely manner, and she is now healthy. We believe it may be a result of her rapid growth. She has the anatomy of a normal baby girl, but she continues to grow significantly faster than normal. We did a full body scan, and it seems the brain is struggling to keep up with the rest of the body. We will monitor this issue closely to see if it persists. In any case, the incident has helped me realize how much I care about her. She is like the daughter I never had. She was conceived from my tissue samples, so I guess technically she *is* my daughter. After learning that I was sterile, I gave up on the possibility of passing on my legacy, but this changes everything.

Day 105   Weight: 19 pounds   Length: 28 inches
Today Isabella said "dada" for the first time. I was holding her in my arms, and she said it while looking into my eyes. I never realized how much I've wanted to be a father until we began this experiment. Every time I look at her, I see all of the best parts of myself. She's perfect in every way.

Day 123 · Weight: 20 pounds Length: 29 inches
Isabella's legs are now strong enough to support her own weight. She can walk with little to no assistance. It is exciting to watch her play. She is a bundle of joy, bunched into one tiny person.

She is still developing unusually fast. Her seizures have persisted, but have caused no danger to her health. We have learned how to deal with them. To ensure her safety, we place her on her back, away from any obstacles, and gently hold her head in place. The seizures average about thirty seconds to a minute in duration. We still believe it is due to the abnormally rapid development of her brain.

Day 158 Weight: 23 pounds Length: 32 inches
Isabella is learning more words. She cannot yet speak in full sentences, but it is amazing how much she knows already. She is not even a half year old. It is all going by so fast. I am excited right now, but I worry that if she continues to grow at this pace, she will suffer a shorter life. She may even pass before I do. No father should watch their child die.

Day 194   Weight: 27 pounds   Height: 34 inches
It is such a joy to watch Isabella play. She is more energetic than ever. Watching her play reminds me of a better time in my life. Being a kid was simpler. No worries. No responsibilities. No vices. Just an innocent ball of joy. Things really change when you get older.

Day 283   Weight: 32 pounds   Height: 37 inches
I didn't think Isabella could get more energetic, but I was wrong. She's started climbing furniture, which makes me nervous, especially with her seizures. Maybe I worry too much, but that's what parents do. Her seizures are always scary, but we can easily keep her from hurting herself. She occasionally bites the tip of her tongue, but we have learned that applying a light pressure under the joint of her lower jaw prevents this.

Her speech has improved drastically in the last few weeks. She could recently only speak in two or three word phrases. Now she is forming full sentences with a robust vocabulary. She is also very organized. I saw her earlier this week sorting her toys by size and color.

Day 365   Weight: 34 pounds   Height: 40 inches
It has only been a year, but Isabella has the appearance of a four-year-old. She has physically grown a lot, and her cognitive abilities far surpass that of a one-year-old. It is exciting to see how far she has come in such a short time. She has recently taken an interest in drawing. Her drawings are basic, but I adore every one of them. She drew a picture of me holding her hand the other day. I posted it up in my office.

Day 414   Weight: 40 pounds   Height: 43 inches
Today Isabella told me she wants to go by Izzy. How can I say no to that adorable face? Izzy it is! It will take some time to get used to, after calling her Isabella for over a year, but it does sound nice.

Day 465   Weight: 44 pounds   Height: 46 inches
Somehow, Izzy has managed to find more energy! She can barely sit still for even a minute and constantly asks questions about everything. She keeps on asking if she can leave the labs and go outside. I try to explain that it's dangerous for her. She nods her head, but I think she still wants to leave. I don't blame her. Being stuck in these labs would drive me crazy too. It tears me up to say no to her, but it's necessary. I can't risk anyone seeing her. I

have brought her up to my office a few times to show her the view from my window. Her face lights up every time.

We have performed another body scan to monitor the development of her condition. We found some sort of mutation on the back of her brain. It does not appear harmful, and in fact, seems to be helping. Her seizures still persist, but are now far less frequent. I believe the mutation is affecting her rate of growth as well. It has somehow managed to slow her aging. She continues to grow faster than a normal child, but these results are still hard to ignore. This could possibly lead to exciting new breakthroughs in the vitality sector. If the mutation can slow Izzy's growth, what could it do for a normal human being? This is a question I am eager to answer, but unfortunately, we cannot get a closer look without performing brain surgery; something I am not willing to risk. The odds of her death are too high.

Day 553   Weight: 50 pounds   Height: 48 inches
Izzy spends more time with me in my office nowadays. She likes it better than the labs, and I enjoy her company. No one else comes up here, so I don't see the harm in letting her stay.

It's funny. Considering how talkative she is around me, she is very shy around the labbies. She barely says a word to them, and if I'm nearby, she hides behind me. I guess she's shy at heart.

Day -   Weight: -   Height: -

I am writing this in haste. I fear this may be my last entry. The Spire is under attack. Simon has breached the third wall, and his men are storming in. I have issued an emergency. All of my workers should be in the safe rooms, hopefully away from danger. Regretfully, I do not think there are enough evacuation pods for everyone. I will bring Izzy to the pod in my office, but first I wanted to write this last entry. I should have had the courage to share Izzy with others. I was a coward. I let Simon's savagery get the better of me. By the time anyone finds this, Izzy and I will be away, safe from danger. We are leaving the City and never coming back. No one will see the angel that I have created, but they should know she exists. That is why I am leaving this message. To whoever finds this journal, announce it to the world. Make sure everyone knows that a miracle happened. That miracle is Izzy. People deserve to know. Victor Greene, signing off.

P.S. Screw you, Simon.

SEVENTEEN

THEY WERE ALL speechless. Processing the information was overwhelming. They stood in silence, trying to figure out what it meant for them.

"Wait," Alan said, stepping back from the desk. "I'm confused. Is Izzy Greene's daughter?"

"He certainly loved her like a daughter," Charlotte said, flipping to the back cover. There was a picture of Izzy's face sewn into the inner sleeve. She clamped it shut and placed it back on the desk.

"She's an experiment," Vince said. "Like me."

"I had no idea Greene had a secret project," Charlotte said. "He's been hiding it for two years. Hiding *her* for two years."

"Only three people knew about her," Vince said. "Greene, Humphrey, and this Trish Beaumont."

"Two of them are dead," Alan said. "Rest in peace Humphrey. You were a good man."

"Trish Beaumont," Charlotte repeated. "That sounds familiar. Where have I heard that name?"

"She spoke at the ceremony," Vince said.

"I have so many questions," Alan said. "We should find her and squeeze some answers out."

Charlotte walked back to Greene's control panel. "Finding Izzy is priority. Once she's safe, we can track down Trish Beaumont."

"Don't forget about Simon," Vince added.

Charlotte scrolled through the logs on the screen. "Simon and Izzy are most likely together. If we find her, we find him." She sorted the list by date and time, placing the most recent logs on top. "They're using labbie key cards to get around. It looks like they brought us to the cell room, and then headed up to the labs on Level 149."

"We were just there," Alan said. "How did we miss them?"

"The lab area is big. You only saw a small portion of it. There were dozens of vitality experiments taking place all at once."

"And Project Monika was one of them," Vince said.

Charlotte clicked the camera icon to show the security footage. They saw an empty room with a bare wooden desk against the far wall. A mug sat on the surface, but nothing else. The top corner of the screen read *Vitality Lab No. 88.*

"There's no one there," she said. "Let's try this."

The label changed to *Operation Room No. 88,* and the view switched to a room full of people.

"What are they doing in there?" Alan asked.

Charlotte moved the image around, zooming in and panning the camera to get a better angle. "There are so many people, it's hard to tell. We'll have to go down to find out."

"Is it possible to delete the records of Snow Peak?" Alan asked. "I don't like knowing they can spy on us."

"Yes, I can do that." She searched for Snow Peak and a full list of records popped up. "Everything?"

Alan nodded. "Everything."

She clicked a trash icon and the list rapidly shrunk until it was gone. A small window popped up. *Records Permanently Deleted.* Next, she returned to the camera systems and again searched for Snow Peak. She clicked a red icon, and another window popped up. *Cameras Permanently Disabled.*

Alan slung his bag over his shoulder. "Great. Now back to the elevator to rescue the girl."

Vince grabbed the monitor journal from the desk and stuck it in his bag. "This may be useful."

They rode the elevator back down to level 149 and trudged through the hallway towards the labs. They covered their mouths, stepping over the maggot-ridden flesh piles. Alan tried not to look down, in fear that he might gag.

When they reached the entrance to the labs, Charlotte held a finger up to her lips again. "Whispers."

Vince and Alan nodded.

Just like before, Charlotte knew her way through the complex system of hallways. They came across a patrolling guard and knelt in the shadow of a wall. The guard strolled down the hall and reached the far end, before turning around making his way back. They waited in the darkness, staying perfectly still. Perfectly silent. Perfectly invisible. When the guard passed, they slipped out unnoticed, moved down the hall, and swiftly turned the corner.

Charlotte tiptoed to a door and pointed inside. It was *Lab No. 88*. Vince and Alan pressed against the side of the door and gave a thumbs up. She slowly approached the door, waiting for the scanner to pick up her key card. With one more step the door slid open and they entered the empty room.

It was in the same condition that it was in on the camera footage. Nothing of importance. Just a desk holding an engraved turtle mug. She signaled to the back corner, where a sign hung above a doorway. *Operation Room*. There were muffled voices coming from inside.

Again, Vince and Alan pressed against the side of the door, guns clasped tightly in their hands. Charlotte listened to the voices, but could not make out who they were.

There was no way for them to sneak in. The door would automatically open once she reached its proximity. They were relying on the element of surprise. She held up three fingers. Three. Two. One.

She charged at the door as it slid open, gun raised and ready to fire. Vince and Alan slipped in behind her, covering the right and left corners.

Simon glanced up, startled. There were seven others in the room. Trish Beaumont sat in the back. One of the three guards was pointing a gun at her head. The other two pointed at Simon's. Jonah stood at the far right, flashing his crooked teeth with a smile. Another man stood over the operating table, in what was unmistakably a doctor's uniform.

On the table, was Izzy. She lay face up, unconscious with a plastic mask pumping gas into her lungs. Various wires latched to her body, connected to a tall stack of machines that constantly beeped.

Vince glared at Simon with expected hatred. The man who killed his oldest friend, right in front of his eyes. The blood boiled in his veins.

Simon sighed with relief. "Finally. You took your sweet time getting here." He pointed to Crooked Tooth. "Jonah here decided to grow a pair."

Jonah looked at the three of them, standing in the doorway. "How did you get out of your cells?"

"The power was off, you idiot," Alan said. "It was easy as pie."

"Put an end to this," Simon said pointing to Jonah. "Shoot him."

Alan looked at Simon in pure amazement. "Why in the world would we help you?"

"Are you blind? He has your girl. He's going to cut her head open."

Vince kept his glare on Simon, his temper rising.

Jonah waved a dismissive hand. "Don't listen to him. He doesn't know what he's talking about. His vision for the City is all screwy. Greene was a problem for me, but I do believe in many of the things he did. These tests are one of them. They enhance people's lives." He pointed to Simon. "This nut wants to end all of that. He wants to stop the tests forever. He says Greene went too far with his tests, but I say he didn't go far enough. He wasn't reaching his full potential."

"See what I mean?" Simon said. "He's gone mad."

"Shut up!" Jonah yelled, spraying a mist of spit across the room. "I've put up with your nonsense long enough, but no more." He pointed to the guards. "They're aiming their guns at you. That means I'm in charge. You're not calling the shots anymore."

"What are you doing to her?" Charlotte asked.

Jonah smiled. "I'm glad you asked. You see, she is the perfect example of lost potential. You may not know this, but Izzy is a very special girl. You see, her brain has mutated in ways which we can benefit from. Greene was chasing immortality. He made many great strides in the field of longevity, but he never quite reached his goal. We are so close, and she," he pointed to Izzy, "is the key to it all. We just need to slice open her head and see what makes that brain tick. Greene was too soft to make that sacrifice."

Trish shook her head and called out from the back. "You're a sadistic monster."

Jonah raised his palms over his head. "Hey, I'm just doing what you said. I'm continuing Greene's work. That was a beautiful speech, by the way. Very inspiring."

"Don't you dare twist my words to justify whatever this is."

"I don't *have* to justify anything. This is going to happen whether you like it or not. I don't need your approval."

Charlotte and Alan moved in with their guns raised. The guards moved forward to block their way, aiming their guns directly at their heads.

"I wouldn't do that if I were you," Jonah said. "These guards aren't afraid to kill. I mean, just look at that hallway out there. A real mess." He wandered over to looked down at Izzy. "You know, when I woke up this morning, I had no idea I would be blessed with this gift. After we found Greene's journal, we knew we had to find her. We needed the only person alive who knew she existed. Trish Beaumont. That's why we were out there in the first place. That's why we attacked the ceremony. Not in the slightest did I expect to find the very girl herself. But here we are. I guess luck is in my favor."

"Luck runs thin with traitors," Simon said. "This girl isn't a slave to these tests. She should be free to do as she pleases."

Vince ignored his words. Their interests aligned at the moment, but rage clouded his mind.

Jonah placed a hand on the doctor's shoulder. "Please, continue. They won't disrupt you."

The doctor grabbed a scalpel and nodded. "She's ready. I am making the first incision." He raised the scalpel up and pressed against Izzy's forehead.

Vince lunged at Simon and grabbed him by the neck. One arm squeezed his throat, and the other covered his mouth. They all jumped with surprise at the sudden outburst. The guards swung their guns to point at Vince.

Jonah tilted his head, puzzled. "You know, that doesn't give you much leverage." He chuckled. "I don't care if he lives or dies. Go ahead, kill him."

"He deserves to die," Vince said. His words were spaced between large breaths of anger. "He's killed so many. He killed Saul."

"I am truly sorry about that," Jonah said with cheer. "If there's one thing I've learned from working with Simon, he's one hell of a wild card."

"He deserves it," Vince repeated, breathing heavily. "He deserves it. He deserves it."

Alan and Charlotte shared a nervous glance.

Vince's muscles tensed, and the small tendrils emerged from his pores, hungry. Simon's eyes shot open when he realized what was happening. He twisted and turned, but struggling only tightened the grip around his neck. He opened his mouth, but his cries for help were muffled by Vince's hand. His eyes darted back and forth until pain shot instantly through his body. His muscles lost control, and his eyes rolled into his skull.

Vince held Simon's body firm, restricting even the smallest of struggles. His face was full of blood-fueled rage. Everything Simon had done. Everyone Simon had killed. At this moment, he would pay for it all. He would pay for Saul. His payment, a painful death.

He sucked the life through Simon's skin, the power surging into his body. It was a power he had never felt before. The energy of a human being. It was overwhelming at first, but he quickly embraced it.

Simon lurched from side to side before finally going limp. Vince released his grip and let the body fall. He looked up at the others, with heavy breaths. A smile covered his face. Adrenaline pumped through his veins, shooting pleasure throughout his body.

Jonah examined Simon's corpse and then peered up at Vince. "Very impressive. We'll have to study you as well." He signaled to the guards. "Get him boys."

The guards moved in. With renewed energy running through his chest, Vince felt unstoppable. He slammed his fist into the jaw of the first guard and threw his shoulder at the second one. They stumbled back and then charged in again. The third guard raised his gun.

"Don't shoot him, you moron. I need him alive."

The guard lowered his gun and joined the others, kneeing Vince in the stomach. Vince grabbed his leg and swung him into the wall. Fists swung into his face and drew blood from his mouth. He wiped it away and swung back with a fury of hits. One of them drew a rod from his belt and flipped a switch on the handle. A bright spark flashed from the tip. He held it forward and thrust it into Vince's leg.

Vince's muscled tightened as the current shot through his body. He froze in place, unable to move, glaring at Jonah with furious eyes. When the guard finally lifted the rod, he fell to the ground like a sack of potatoes, motionless.

"Vince!" Charlotte yelled.

Alan was too shocked to speak.

Jonah chuckled. "Again, very impressive. He took on three fully trained guards and put up a pretty good fight." He looked back to Izzy. "Anyway, where were we? Oh right. You were just about to cut into her scalp. I'm itching to see what's inside."

The doctor glanced at Jonah, nodded, and lifted the scalpel for another try.

"No!" Charlotte yelled. She raised her gun and pulled the trigger. The doctor's hand exploded in blood as the bullet cut clean through his palm. He dropped the scalpel and grabbed his wrist.

A guard turned in one swift motion and shot Charlotte straight through the head. Alan dropped his gun and fell back in a stupor, with Charlotte's blood splashed across his face. He stumbled through the doorway and ran for the exit. The guards started to follow, but Jonah raised his hand.

"Let him go. He's not coming back. We've got business to do here." He examined the doctor's hand. It was spurting blood as he grabbed it with the other. "Damn it, now we can't operate!" He marched over to Charlotte's dead body and knelt down. "Because of you, now we have to find another doctor. I hope you're happy."

He stood up and patted the doctor's back. "You'll be fine. You won't be performing surgeries any time soon, but you'll live." He clapped his hands together. "Well, I guess this project is postponed." He pointed to Charlotte. "Clean up this mess. Lock these three up in the cell room. And make sure the power is on this time, damn it!"

EIGHTEEN

R UPERT AND ELLA sat at the dinner table, joined by Charlotte's friend, Trevor. They munched on a hearty vegetable stew, prepared by Rupert himself. Ella stared at the table, pushing her food around the edge of her bowl.

Rupert glanced at her. "Is something on your mind?"

She did not respond and continued to play with her food.

"Ella?"

She flinched and looked up to see who called her name. "I'm sorry, what?"

"Is something on your mind? You seem distracted."

"It's just a feeling I have. Something is wrong. I don't know why, but I feel like Alan and the others are in trouble."

"Of course they're in trouble," Trevor said, shoveling stew down his throat. "They charged into a place full of people that hate them. What did they expect?"

"So why didn't you stop them from leaving?" Ella asked, frustrated. "Charlotte's your friend, isn't she?"

"Yes, a good friend, but she can think for herself. It was their decision to go back. Who am I to say if it was the right or wrong decision? They had their reasons to leave, and we had ours to stay."

"But you knew their lives were in danger. It's your responsibility to stop them, or at least try." She looked to Rupert for help, but he only shrugged.

"Hey," Trevor said, scraping the bottom of his bowl. "I'm safe and sound in this village. As far as I'm concerned, that's all that matters." He eyed her bowl. "Are you going to finish that?"

She shoved her bowl off the table and shot up from her seat. "You're such a pig, Trevor. Quit eating for one second and think about someone other than yourself."

Trevor raised his hands in the air. "I'm not selfish. I'm just being honest. There is no way we would have convinced them to stay. They already made up their minds. At least Charlotte did. I've worked with her for a few decades. I know how she thinks. The City is her home, no matter how dangerous. I, on the other hand, want home to be safe. Apparently, you do too. Otherwise, you would have gone with them. We're not being selfish, just reasonable."

Ella glared with wide eyes and sat down again. She hated to admit it, but he was right. They had all made their own decisions. Now she was questioning hers. Maybe she should have gone back with them. To her, home was where your family was. Whatever dangers they faced, they would face it as a family, but instead, they split up. Ella sat comfortably in Snow Peak, but her comfort was hindered by a feeling of regret. She could see it in Rupert's face as well.

"Let's go back," she said. "Let's find them and help."

Trevor shook his head. "I'm not going."

She ignored Trevor. "Rupert, let's go help them."

Rupert considered her words and then nodded. "If we can help our friends, we should at least try."

A long smile stretched across her face.

Trevor eyed the bowl of stew that Ella had pushed to the ground. Some was still in the bowl and had not touched the floor. "How are you going to get there?"

"Shoot," she said. "That's right, they took the boat."

"The evacuation pods," Rupert said. "You came here in one. We can take one back."

Trevor shook his head. "Those things aren't designed for long distance. We had enough trouble getting them as far as we did. There's no way you'll make it back in one."

Ella lowered her head. "Without a motorized boat, we can't get back. We could go on a raft, but that would take weeks. Maybe even months."

"And we can't fit more than a week's worth of supplies on a raft," Rupert said.

"So what do we do?" She asked, looking back at Rupert and Trevor. She knew the answer, but she asked anyway, hoping they would have a miraculous solution.

"I'm afraid there isn't much we *can* do," Rupert said.

She lowered her head and stared at the table. Their friends were in danger. She could feel it in her gut, but there was nothing they could do.

NINETEEN

ALAN'S HEART POUNDED in his chest as he ran down the halls. He no longer minded the awful smell rising from the dead. He was more concerned with not dying himself. He raced down the corridor, flailing his arms and panting.

He turned the corner and stopped to catch his breath. When he peeked back around the corner, there was no one there. Just a hallway full of bodies. He had lost them. Or they let him go. Either way, he was still alive.

He stumbled to the elevator, unable to think straight. His head was spinning with overwhelming confusion. He entered the elevator and pressed Level 1. The moment the doors closed, he bent over and threw up in the corner.

Charlotte was dead. Vince and Izzy were captured. Now he was on his own. What should he do? Run? Hide in the streets and hope they never find him? Go back up to rescue Vince and Izzy? Or return to Snow Peak?

Yes. That was the only reasonable option. Return to Snow Peak. But he refused to leave his friends behind, trapped in a cell. He would return to Snow Peak and plead for Ella and Rupert to help him. He couldn't do it alone, but with the help of others, he might be able to pull it off.

But how would he get back? He did not know the way to the docks, and their raft was long gone.

Then he remembered what Charlotte said. The Spire had its own dock. It would be on the lowest level, below Level 1. He pressed the cancel button and instead hit Level 0. There he would grab a boat and sail back home. That was the plan. Grab a boat. Get Ella and Rupert. Come back. Rescue Vince and Izzy. What could possibly go wrong?

Of course, he knew *everything* could go wrong. The boats might not start. Ella and Rupert might not come with him. They might be too late. It would probably take him at least two weeks to get there and come back. But that would not stop him from trying.

He wiped the chunks from his mouth and stood tall, ready to run once it the doors opened. He would not waste time. Not a single second. When the doors opened, he would sprint to the dock as fast as he could.

The elevator beeped and the doors slid open. He dashed out, but quickly realized he did not know his way to the docks.

"Crap!" he yelled, and then covered his mouth, remembering that guards might be around. There was an interactive map on the opposite wall. He ran up and tapped the screen furiously. He found Level 0, and then the docks. Down the hall. Two rights and a left. He hit the wall with his fist, and ran down the hall, repeating the turns in his head. Down the hall. Two rights and a left.

No one was around. Level 0 was deserted. That was good news for Alan. No obstacles. No distractions. No one to stop him. He took a sharp right, and the salty scent of sea water entered his nostrils. Another right. The horrific scene was stuck in his head. Charlotte falling over in an explosion of blood. Vince shaking furiously as electricity surged through his body. Izzy lying helplessly on that operating table. These images flashed in his mind and pushed him to move even faster. The tip tap of his feet was overtaken by the sound of waves, crashing into the Spire walls. He took a quick left.

Around the corner was the large dock. It stood even larger than the Western Gate, but he had no time to awe over the vast space. He needed to find a boat, but which one? He hoped for a fast one, but he could only guess. His eyes filtered through each one, studying his options. There were so many, it was impossible to choose.

Instead of wasting more time, he pointed to the one nearby. "That one," he said. It was as good of a guess as any. He trotted up and hopped in. It was smaller than the others. Not quite as large as the one they arrived in. There was no pantry. No bedroom. No lounge. There was only one floor with one room. The control room. It was all he needed.

He tinkered with the controls. He had watched Charlotte steer before, but this was different. The buttons and levers were jumbled around. He examined the panel, studying each one until he found what he was looking for. He slammed on the button and heard the motor start.

He gripped the lever and carefully pushed forward. A maze of boats stood in his way. He maneuvered through, resisting the urge to push the throttle to the limit. He would not be helpful to anyone trapped in a pile of boat wreckage. He restrained his hand until he made it through the gate, and then pushed it up as high as it would go. The motor growled and the boat jerked forward, moving at a steady pace.

Alan looked down at the water. "Is that all you got?" He pushed more buttons and grabbed more levers. The motor pushed from a growl to a roar and the boat jerked forward with unexpected speed.

"That's what I'm talking about!" he yelled. "Don't worry Vince, help is on the way."

TWENTY

TRISH STARED AT Charlotte's body as the guards dragged her out. A long streak of blood trailed behind. She then looked at Vince, unconscious on the ground, still shaking from the powerful shock that was sent through his body. Both of them were traitors. Greene trusted them, and they stabbed him in the back. The City was in shambles, and they were to blame.

She moved her eyes to Izzy, who was motionless on the table. The girl was back in the City, and she was alive. Trish looked back to Vince with curious confusion. She had thought he was working with Simon, but for reason's she could not explain, he attacked him. He drained his energy and ended his life. From the rage she saw in his eyes, it was obvious he hated the man.

And then Charlotte saved Izzy. The girl was Greene's flesh and blood, but the woman who led Greene to his death also saved Izzy from hers. She sacrificed her own life to save her enemy's daughter.

They were people she believed to be traitors. They were responsible for the death of her friends, but now they were helping for reasons she could not explain. Thinking about it made her head spin.

Jonah snapped his fingers and pointed to Izzy. "Get the girl off the table and lock her up with the rest of them. We can't do the surgery anymore. Not until we find another doctor." He approached the doctor, who was grasping his bloody wrist. "You are free to go."

The doctor was trembling, his face soaked in tears. "I need medical attention. Get someone to help me."

"I'm afraid I don't have the resources. Consider it lucky I'm letting you live in the first place. If it were up to Simon, you would already be dead. But I'm a nice guy. I'm letting you go. You'll be fine. You're a doctor. You'll figure it out."

"I can't treat myself," he pleaded. "I need someone to stitch me up. It hurts so much. I can't even hold still." He held out his hand, and it shook beyond his control.

Jonah shook his head. "Sorry doc. It's not my problem. I've already paid you for nothing. You didn't complete your job, but I'm letting you go anyway. You're stretching it. Get out of my face before I change my mind. And to make sure my money doesn't completely go to waste, head upstairs and switch on the power in the cell room. I got to make you work at least a little. Otherwise, I'm just throwing money down the drain."

The doctor glanced at him for a moment longer and shambled out of the room with a lowered head.

Jonah looked to Trish, who averted her eyes. "Why so nervous, honey? I'm not going to hurt you if you cooperate. We know everything we need to about that girl so far, but if the time comes and we need your help, I expect you to answer our questions honestly. Do that, and you have nothing to worry about. You're the only one alive who knew about Greene's daughter. It would be a shame if that were no longer the case."

Trish continued to avoid eye contact. Instead, she focused her eyes on Izzy. "She doesn't deserve this."

"Of course she doesn't deserve this, but sometimes life is unfair. Trust me, a lot of good will come from this. Her death will lead to great things."

She continued staring at the girl, considering what to say next.

"If you don't cooperate," Jonah said, "I'm afraid there's no reason for me to keep you alive."

"You could just let me go, like the doctor."

He shook his head. "That doctor was willing to help. He was just put in an unfortunate circumstance. You, on the other hand, have not helped me or hurt me. You have yet to make a decision. If you choose to help me, then you're an asset. I will take care of you. But if you choose not to help me, I can only assume you intend to hurt me. That is something I can't ignore. I can't let someone like that go free. You'll just come back later and bite me in the ass." He looked at his hand and noticed a splotch of blood that had splattered onto his palm. He wiped it away with the tip of his thumb. "So, what will it be? Help me, or hurt me?"

She took her eyes from Izzy and moved them to Jonah. "Help you," she whispered.

Jonah leaned in. "I'm sorry, what did you say?"

"I will help you. Ask whatever you'd like about the girl and I will answer. However, I will not harm the girl in any way. I will only provide information."

Jonah smiled. "Fair enough." He looked up at his guards. "Why are you taking so long? You don't need to clean every last inch. Just leave her body there. She's not going anywhere. She's got a hole in her face for Christ's sake. She's out of the room. That's good enough. Now get back in here and lock up our prisoners before they wake up."

The guards dropped Charlotte and moseyed back in. One lifted Izzy in his arms. Another walked up to Trish and spun her around.

"Please," she said, "you don't need to cuff me. I'm not going to run."

The guard glanced at Jonah, who nodded. He shrugged back and joined the third to help carry Vince. Jonah grabbed his turtle mug off the desk, before following the others out. He walked beside Trish, taking careful sips of tea.

He looked over as he walked. "You know, if it were up to me, things wouldn't have happened the way they did. I would not have killed your coworkers. Of course, Greene's soldiers were a threat that needed to be dealt with, but the labbies were different. I have no reason to kill your kind. In fact, you are of great value to me. After all, I intend to continue the tests. That requires labbies."

Trish said nothing. She looked straight ahead and followed the guards as they entered the cell room.

"I also need test subjects," he continued. "I should have acted sooner, before Simon set them free. Now I have to gather them back up. The only good that came from the attack was Greene's death. He needed to move aside so someone could take his place. Someone with guts to do what it takes."

"And you think that person is you?" Trish asked.

"I do. I don't expect you to believe it right now, but in time, you will. You'll see the wasted potential that slipped through Greene's fingers. He was on the right track, but he needed to grow a pair."

Their feet clanged on the metal grating as they descended the stairs to the lower levels. Jonah watched Trish as he talked, trying to gauge her reaction. She showed none.

"Simon, on the other hand, needed to tone it down. He was extremely passionate, which is something I admire, but his passion was for the wrong reasons. Fortunately, I was able to channel that passion into something useful. We never would have broken through the walls without him."

"You owe the world to Vince," Trish said. "Without him, Simon never would have succeeded."

Jonah nodded. "I suppose that's true. I'll remember to thank him when he wakes. Both for helping Simon, and for killing him. I would have done it myself, but now I don't have to."

"What are you going to do next?"

"I've already told you. I plan to continue Greene's work. The first step is to find another doctor so we can get a good look at this girl's brain. She will be the first test under my belt. After that, we must expand. I have already started to gather more subjects. They're scattered throughout the City, but we're sniffing them out."

"Your guards are okay with that?" Trish asked. "Just a moment ago they were fighting to free the test subjects. Now they're gathering them back up? Why would they do that?"

"That is one of my biggest concerns, and I currently don't have a solution. I have my loyal group of guards right here. They truly believe in my vision. There are a few others in the Spire, but the majority of the Crowns support Simon's vision. It completely contradicts mine. Right now, they are cooperating because they think the orders are coming directly from Simon. They trust that his orders have meaning and that it's part of his master plan. They don't know I've taken control, but they will soon catch on. It's only a matter of time. I'm hoping the results of this test with the girl will help sway some of them. If I'm lucky, it will convert enough to outnumber the rest. If it doesn't, Simon is dead so they won't have a leader. At least not at first. I can use that time to my advantage."

"I don't think that will work," Trish said.

"It is risky, I'll admit, but I do believe it will work." They moved away from the staircase and walked up to the cells. "This is where the three of you will stay until I find a replacement doctor."

The guards placed Vince and Izzy in the cell, both propped up against the wall.

Trish glanced into the cell, and then to Vince. "Wait, you're putting us all in the same cell?"

Jonah nodded. "Why not?"

"I can't be locked in with *him*. He's a traitor. He is responsible for the death of my friends. I can't stand to look at him for another second."

"Suck it up. We can't all get what we want. You're lucky enough that I'm keeping you alive." He nudged her forward, but she resisted.

"No! I will not."

Jonah sighed. "Fine. You can have this cell." He opened the one to the right.

"I want to be on a different level."

"For Christ's sake, I don't have time for this. Just get in the cell."

"No. I demand to be on my own level, far away from him."

"You're in no position to be making demands. Now get in the damn cell." He pushed her forward.

She spun around and slapped him in the face. "You said you want me to help. I will be more helpful if I'm happy. I will not be happy if I'm anywhere near this scum. Give me my own level and I'll make things much easier for you."

Jonah pressed a palm against his cheek, which was turning red, and smiled. "I like you. You're bold." He looked to his guards. "Escort her a few levels up."

"The girl, too," she said. "The girl comes with me."

"You're pushing your luck, lady. You're bold, but you don't know when to stop. I'm feeling generous, but not that generous. The girl stays."

"You can't leave her with that monster."

"I can do whatever I want. I'm in charge, remember? I make the calls. If I say the girl stays, the girl stays." He waved his hand to the guards.

They closed the cell door and dragged Trish up the stairs. Jonah watched as she disappeared into darkness. He stayed behind and glared at his unconscious prisoners. A wide smile stretched across his face. "You may have bought some time, but sit tight. Your time will come. As soon as I find another doctor, we'll slice you up nice and good."

He grabbed the bars and shook with force. The door swung freely. The power had not been restored.

He crossed his arms. "Damn it doc! You pay a man to do a job, and he hits the ground running. Well, that was money down the drain."

TWENTY-ONE

VINCE WOKE UP in the same cell again. This time, it was different, though. Izzy was locked in with him. He looked across the catwalk at the kiosk. The light on the panel was still out. They had not turned on the power. He walked to the door and kicked it as he had before, but this time, it did not budge. He leaned over to see a mechanical lock wrapped around the bars. They must have had trouble turning the power on.

Jonah wandered up on the catwalk and peered inside the cell. "I wondered how long you would be out. Those shockers are pretty nasty, huh?" He wrapped his fingers around the bars and pulled. The door held firmly in place. "You're not getting out this time, so make yourself comfortable. It will be a while before we find another doctor. It's delicate work to remove organs. We wouldn't want to damage them."

Vince stood up, but did not say a word.

"You're shy, aren't you? Both of you. Either that or you just don't like me. Trust me, I'm a good guy. I know when I owe someone. You killed Simon for me. For that I thank you."

He paused to let Vince respond, but he still remained silent.

"Still nothing? I can't blame you. It's better than that labbie. She wouldn't shut up about you. Just kept on going on about how you're a traitor and a disgrace to the Spire. Yap, yap, yap. I had to put her on her own level just to shut her mouth. But you, both of you, are easy." He tapped his fingers against the metal. "Well, I've got some work to do. We need to find a new doctor." He walked away and out of sight. "Don't get *too* comfortable," he said, walking away.

Vince glanced at Izzy, who stared back at him. "How long was I out?" he asked.

She playfully rocked back and forth. "Three hours maybe."

"Where are Charlotte and Alan?"

She shook her head and shrugged.

He pressed his palms into his face and fell back against the wall, sliding down until he was sitting. He took a deep breath and sighed. "What is wrong with me?"

Izzy walked by his side. "What do you mean?" she asked.

"I drained a human," He shook his head. "I said I would stop, but it's only gotten worse."

"Stop what?" Izzy asked.

He stared straight ahead. "It's a long story. You wouldn't understand." He held out his hand to see the microscopic tendrils poking out from his skin. From a distance, they looked like hairs, but up close they were grotesque. "I'm stuck in an endless cycle, and I'm so tired."

Izzy stared at him, but did not say a word. He did not expect her to. He patted down his clothes to see what they had taken. His knives and guns were all gone, but there was something in his cloak pocket. He reached in and pulled out a capsule. The poison. He held it in front of his face, turning it in his fingers.

Izzy wandered the cell and strummed the bars with her fingers. "What are they going to do to me?"

Vince slipped the pill back in his pocket and looked up. He didn't have the heart to tell her to truth. "They're going to test you. Me as well."

"Why do they want to test me?"

"You're one of Greene's test subjects. Both of us are."

"Test subjects? He doesn't test me, though. He's my daddy."

Vince admired her innocence. She had started as a test subject, but she grew into something much more. There was no doubt that Greene loved her, but had he really abandoned his plans to test on her? The monitor journal expressed much love for his *daughter*. It was hard to imagine he would treat her like his other subjects.

"I don't want to test," she said.

"I'm afraid we don't have a choice." This part he said with genuine sorrow. There was no chance of escaping. They had been lucky so many times, they were due for some misfortune. The girl would certainly die. Vince's future was a less certain, but it was not promising.

He sat against the wall, staring straight ahead. A tear fell from his eye.

TWENTY-TWO

ALAN KEPT HIS hand on the throttle, pushing forward even though it was already at full speed. The boat cut through waves with impressive speed. The coast appeared on the horizon. He was making good time. A trip that previously took several days was reduced to just one, but he was still anxious. He wanted to go faster. The girl's life depended on it.

He approached the shore, only slightly reducing his speed. When the boat hit land, he cut the motor. The boat wedged through the sandy beach and slid to a halt. He jumped on shore and ran across the beach. Clouds of sand kicked up behind him as he dashed towards the cave. Inside the hollow cavern, the sound of his footsteps bounced off the walls. The horrible stench he had tried to forget came rushing back with a wave of memories. The pile of bodies was still in place, with Barnabus' corpse stuck beside it.

He glared at the cage that encompassed the pool of dismembered flesh. The goo-like substance was dripping off the edge, covering the seat and controls of the vehicle. He examined the motor attached to the front and recalled what Charlotte had said. The walk to Snow Peak was five days, but the cage would cut that in half. Alan was repulsed by the idea of dealing with the bodies, but matters were urgent. He could not bear to ride with the mess in the back. His only option was to clear it off.

"Damn it, Charlotte. Quit being right all the time."

He rolled up his sleeves and tightened the scarf around his face. The smell was still strong, but it helped a little. He dug his hands into the pile of mush, and a strange bubbly gas rose up, hissing at the surface. A salty taste rose into the air and entered his mouth. The piercing stench crawled up his nose and made his head spin. He swung around and hunched over, throwing up against the wall. A pool of bile collected at his feet. He stared down at the greenish liquid as it oozed towards his boots. His own vomit was more pleasing to look at than the grotesque gelatinous body pile.

He stepped away for a breath of fresh air, and to regain his composure. Going back in was the last thing he wanted to do, but he knew it was necessary. If he wanted to save his friends, he would have to drive the cage. He turned around and returned to the nauseating sludge pile.

He scooped slops of gelatin in his hands. As he reached the bottom, bones poked out in different directions. At the sight of a spine, he spun around and gagged once more. This time, nothing came out. He had already emptied his stomach the first time. He turned back around and picked out the bones, tossing them to the side.

When the cage was cleared out, he climbed into the front seat and took control. The buttons and levers resembled the controls of the boat. He searched for the ignition button, and when he found it, he slammed his fist down. The motor briefly purred, and then petered out.

He threw up his hands in frustration. "Please don't tell me I cleaned up that mess for nothing!"

He pressed it again, this time holding it down. The purr grew to a light growl and died down once more.

"Come on, damn it!"

He raised up his fists and slammed down on the panel. The motor burst out in a loud roar and leveled off at a steady hum. He sighed with relief and hit the gas. The cage lurched forward and rammed into the wall. The steering felt different than the boat. It would take some time to adjust. He backed away from the wall and carefully steered towards the exit. Once he was out in the open landscape, he revved the motor and sailed through the snow plains, hurtling towards Snow Peak.

TWENTY-THREE

IZZY PACED AROUND the cell. Despite their situation, she was full of energy. She hopped to and fro, trying to entertain herself. "When do you think they'll let us out?" she asked, balancing on one foot and hopping onto the other. "It's been a long time."

Vince watched from the corner. "They're certainly taking their time. They must be having trouble finding another doctor."

They heard the faint call of someone in the distance.

"Who is that?" Izzy asked.

"I don't know, but they've been at it for a while. Is someone else locked up in these cells?"

"There's Trish."

He shook his head. "That's not a woman's voice. Jonah must have found more test subjects."

They sat a while longer, listening to the cry of the distant prisoner.

"I'm bored," Izzy said. "We've been in here for so long."

Vince chuckled. "This is nothing."

"What do you mean?"

"I've been around for over two hundred years. With that many years under your belt, you build patience."

Her face lit up. "Two hundred years?"

"That's right. Two hundred long years."

She stopped pacing and sat next to him. "That's a long time. What do you do? What have you seen?"

"I've seen many things. Oceans, deserts, mountains, valleys. You name it."

Her face glowed with awe. "I want to see it all. I only know the Spire. Daddy never let me leave. I've seen a view of the City from his office, but that's it. I've read books about different places. I can only imagine how beautiful they are."

"You've seen the ocean now. What did you think?"

"It was amazing. The air. The smell. Everything about it was perfect."

Vince nodded. "It was very beautiful. You've seen the beach, and the snow plains as well."

She bounced up and down. "I know. It was so much fun. The sand felt really neat, and the snow was different than I imagined, but I liked it. The trees in the forest were pretty too. They smell really nice."

"Yes, I suppose they do."

"I want to see more. What's the desert like?"

"For the most part, it's miserable. The desert is not a place to get lost."

Izzy shrugged. "I still want to see it. I want to see everything."

"Well, I've seen just about everything in the time I've been given. It loses its thrill after a while."

"Do you get bored?"

He thought about the question. "I get tired."

"Tired of what?"

"Everything. Waking up. Traveling. It's all so tiring."

She looked up with a cheery smile. "Then go to sleep."

"I can't. I have to watch you. It's important that you're safe. I have to protect people like you from people like Simon and Jonah. There are always people like them who need to be watched."

"I'll be okay on my own. You don't need to look after me. We can tag team. I watch you while you sleep and then we switch."

"Tag team?"

"Yeah. You can't stay awake forever. We can take turns."

Vince gave it some thought. He had never considered letting her keep watch, but he saw no reason not to. Still, something about it made him uncomfortable. "I should stay awake. At least for now." He watched her thumbs twiddle about. "You said you're bored? Let's play a game."

She popped up with excitement. "A game? What game?"

"Here, we'll make sentences. I'll say a word, then you say one, and we'll see how the sentence turns out. Ready?"

She nodded and flashed a large smile.

If. I. Had. A. Flying. Dog. My. Life. Would. Be. Complete.

They laughed at the ridiculous sentence they had formed.

"I've always wanted a dog," Izzy said. "I've see pictures, but never one in real life."

"They can't fly," Vince said, snickering to himself. "You know that, right?"

"Yeah, yeah. I know. But a girl can dream. Let's do another one."

"Okay. You start this time."

Whenever. I. Eat. My. Tummy. Tries. To. Escape.

They shared another laughing fit. This sentence was more ridiculous than the last.

"One more," she said. "It's your turn to start."

How. Do. We. Know. What. The. Time. Is. If. You. Don't. Go. To. Sleep.

Vince shot a suspicious glare. "Are you trying to get me to go to sleep?"

"Maybe," she said.

"You're a sneaky one. Okay, you win. I'll sleep for a little bit. Not for too long, though. And when I wake, we'll switch."

"Tag team," she said.

"Right. Tag team."

He took his spot against the wall and stretched his legs. His fixed his eyes on Izzy, who stared back.

"Don't worry. I'll keep watch. I'm good at it. I promise." She spun around and vigilantly peeked through the bars.

"If anyone comes, wake me up."

"Yes, sir."

Vince's eyes drooped as a wave of fatigue washed over him. He did not fight it, but instead, embraced it. After all, he had been through, it was nice to have someone else watch after him. His body slumped over, and sleep took control.

TWENTY-FOUR

THE SUN POKED out from beneath the horizon, as Alan steered the cage to the edge of the woods. He slowed to a stop and hopped to the snow. He gazed into the thick forest. With trees and roots scattered about, there was no room for the cage to fit.

"I guess I'm going on foot from here."

He was exhausted, but he managed a light jog. The snow was hard to run in, but time was important. Puffs of breath blew from his lips with each huff for air. *I should really get in shape*, he thought. He had been awake for almost twenty-four hours. Sleep chased him, trying to pull him down, but he fought it off with all his effort. His joints ached. His head hurt. But he did not care. Lives were at stake.

He hoped to convince Rupert and Ella. He was not so much worried about Rupert. It was Ella who would need persuasion. If she was still sour at Vince, things would be much harder. But she also cared for Vince, regardless of how angry she was. It would take some effort, but he could convince her.

A part of him was excited to return, and the other was terrified. He wanted to see Ella and Rupert. He was sure they would happily welcome him back, but they might also scold him for leaving in the first place. Regardless, he was looking forward to seeing their faces. Fred's, as well.

The sun was now up, and the tree shadows stretched far in front of him, causing a collage of light and dark on the blank canvas of snow. He stepped in the prints from their previous trip, but it was difficult to do so while running. He remembered Barnabus' special snow shoes and regretted leaving them back in the cave. Then, he remembered the vicious wound on Vince's feet and decided his boots were not so bad. It was better than nothing.

He reached the end of the woods and saw the cabins in the distance. Smoke rose from the chimneys, a sign that the cabins were occupied. The Spire folk were settled into their new homes. The vast difference from the City to Snow Peak would have been jarring.

"No more temperature control," Alan said to himself. "Now just good old hand built fires." He moved toward the village, yelling and waving his arms. "Ella! Rupert!"

Ella was chopping wood when she heard him. She looked up and saw him running out of the woods. She wiped the sweat from her brow and glanced back as Rupert stepped out from his cabin. Fred was comfortably perched on his shoulder.

Rupert crossed the road and walked past Ella. "What is this all about?" He marched out and met Alan in the middle. Ella leaned her axe against the wall and followed.

Alan stumbled in the snow and fell to his knees, gasping for air. Rupert bent over and helped him to his feet.

"Alan, you look terrible," Ella said. She studied the streaks of blood on his face, and the deep red stains coating his hands. "Are you okay? You're covered in blood."

His breath leveled out. "It's not my blood. I needed to get here fast, so I cleaned off that bloody cage."

"What's so urgent?" Rupert asked.

"Charlotte's dead. Vince and Izzy are captured."

Ella shook her head. "Simon, that bastard."

"No," he said, "Simon's dead too."

"What?" she exclaimed. "Simon's dead? How?"

"Vince snapped. He went berserk and drained the man."

"If Simon's dead, who locked them up?" Rupert asked.

"Simon's grunt turned on him. Jonah."

"Good old crooked tooth," Ella said.

"He wants to continue the tests, but he needed Greene out of the way. He said Greene was doing things wrong. He was holding back. So now Jonah is taking over, and he's starting with Izzy and Vince. He wants to slice the girl's head open."

"Why would he want Izzy?" Ella asked.

"She's special," Alan said. "I have a feeling you already knew that. We found a journal written by Greene. It says she was an experiment. She was conceived in a lab and raised in a test tube. Her brain has mutated, and Jonah thinks it's the key to immortality or something like that." He shook his head. "You know, I'm getting really sick of this immortal mumbo jumbo."

"He sounds much worse than Greene," Ella said with disgust. "Delusional, even."

"He is."

"What happened to Charlotte?" Rupert asked.

"She saved Izzy, but she didn't make it out. She bought both of them more time, but I don't know how much. That's why we need to hurry. We have to go back and help them. I can't do it on my own. I need my family."

Rupert looked at Ella, "This is something we need to discuss first."

"What is there to discuss?" Alan asked. "Vince is our friend. He needs our help."

"There are things to consider. We already know the City is dangerous. Two of our friends have died. We can't charge in blindly at the risk of losing more people."

"If we don't go back we *will* lose more people. We'll lose Vince. We'll lose Izzy."

"They're not the only ones at stake," Rupert said. He had a natural way of commanding authority. "You could die. Ella could die. That place is a deathtrap and every time we go, someone gets killed."

"I know our track record isn't great," Alan pleaded. His voice was frail in comparison, "but Vince would do the same for us."

"Would he?" Ella asked.

"Of course he would. What are you saying?"

"He let our whole village get murdered," she said. "All he cared about was Greene. He didn't consider us."

"That's not true, and you know it. What about the girl? She doesn't deserve this."

Rupert looked down at his feet. "It is a shame she got dragged into this."

Ella had no answer. She knew Alan was right. They needed to save Izzy. It was something she had argued with herself for the past few days. Not long ago, she yelled at Trevor for not caring, but had since changed her mind. She knew her gut was right. She knew returning to the City would lead to more death, but now Alan's words made sense to her. Regardless of how mad she was at Vince, he was a friend. She could not abandon him.

"If you don't come, I'll go alone," Alan said. "It's the right thing to do. Deep down, I think you already know that."

She met his eyes. "Damn it. Okay, I'll come."

Rupert nodded. "I'm in too."

Alan jumped in the air. "Yes! Come one, let's go. There's no time to waste."

"Let us gather supplies first. I'll pack some food. You look hungry. Ella, go find Trevor and tell him we're leaving. Someone needs to be in charge while we're gone. He's a good candidate. The people already look to him for guidance. And take Fred with you." He handed her off. "She's not coming out with us. Not after what she's been through."

"Right," Ella said, taking Fred and running off.

Alan nodded. "Make it quick. Time is ticking."

TWENTY-FIVE

VINCE KEPT WATCH as Izzy slept. It was the second half of what Izzy had called their *tag team*. He sat against the wall, peering through the bars at the faintly lit void of the cell room. More voices had joined the single distant prisoner. Their cries and nonsense echoed through the hollow core of the room.

He ignored the faded calls from the surrounding cells and pondered about where he was. All of his life events led him to this cell, sitting with the daughter of the man he once hated. What was the point of it all? He had built a specific set of principles, but in a single moment, he threw it all out in a fit of rage. He had vowed to never drain a human, but he drained Simon in an instant.

He could call it revenge or justice, but he knew it was neither. It was something he had been running from his entire life. Something he denied ever existed. It was a fear of death.

For the first time in his life, he knew he was afraid. He was stuck in a loop that would never end. He would never stop draining. If he had no reason, he would make one up. While Saul found comfort in his last moments of life, Vince was not so sure he could do the same. Not if he kept on the same path. Jonah would force him to drain for his tests, and if he escaped, he would drain anyway.

He glanced at Izzy, who was peacefully sleeping at the other end. He pressed his fingers against the pill shaped lump in his pocket. Saul had a bullet lodged in his lung, forcing him to embrace his death. This pill could be Vince's bullet. It could be his unstoppable force that drives him to death. It could finally end the vicious cycle. He reached into his pocket and pulled it out, holding it delicately in his hand.

He rolled it in his palm, watching the powder tumble inside. His arm was shaking against his control. He placed the pill on the ground to his side and glanced back at Izzy. There was nothing he could do. Her life would come to a tragic end at the hands of Jonah. She would die whether he was there or not.

No one would miss his presence. Saul was no longer alive, and he had betrayed the only friends he had left. It was his fault the people of Snow Peak were dead. Everyone was better off without him.

He picked up the capsule, this time firmly, and moved it toward his mouth. He touched the pill to his lips, ready to accept his fate in the afterlife. A tear dribbled from his eye.

Before he could bite down, he heard the sound of movement in front of him. It was Izzy. She was having another seizure, this one more violent than the others. He dropped the pill and trotted over to help her trembling body.

He held her head and applied a gentle pressure to her jaw. Her eyes rolled back, revealing only small glimpses of blue. Frightening sounds came from her mouth as her diaphragm contorted with sporadic movements. Her muscles tightened and relaxed in random patterns, sending her limbs into a flying frenzy.

He had seen it before, but it was still terrifying. The total loss of control sent shivers down his spine. It reminded him of draining. She moved the same way Simon did when he was sucking the life from his body. He pulled his hands away at the sight of her shaking body and then forced himself to bring them back in order to secure her head. He had to remind himself that he was not draining, just helping.

The episode lasted longer than the others. He was starting to worry. If something was truly wrong this time, he did not know what to do. He stared through the bars, deciding if he should call for help. He did not expect anyone to come, but it was worth a try. He opened his mouth, ready to yell, when the contortions finally stopped.

He sighed with tremendous relief. Her limbs lay limp on the ground as her chest heaved with heavy breaths. Her eyes rolled forward and rapidly blinked, collecting moisture in the corners.

When the sight of Vince became clear, she smiled with comfort. He responded with a smile of his own. "Are you okay?"

She could not quite speak yet, but she nodded. He held her close as she slowly recovered. Once she was back to normal, she got to her feet. "Tag team. It's your turn to sleep."

Vince stood up and returned to the corner. "No, I'm no longer tired. You get more rest." He sat in his spot and leaned back. She crawled up next to him and cuddled by his side. Is this what it felt like to be a father? He would never know for sure, but he liked to think it was. He wrapped his arm around her shoulder and pulled her in closer. With his other arm, he scooped the pill off the ground and slipped it back in his pocket.

TWENTY-SIX

ALAN AWOKE FROM a well-deserved nap. The roar of the boat had rattled him in his sleep, but he was too exhausted to care. With his eyes rested and stomach full, he stood up to see Ella and Rupert standing at the controls. The night sky was lit with a faint glow on the horizon.

He stood by Ella, staring straight ahead. "Are you mad at me for leaving?"

"Of course I am," she answered.

"But you understand why I did."

She nodded. "Yes, but I don't agree. The City is not a place to call home."

Alan turned to face her. "You're right."

"I know I'm right. Why couldn't you see that before? If you just listened to me, all of this could have been avoided."

He looked down at his feet. "I couldn't stay in Snow Peak after what happened."

"And the City is better?" she said. "What about all of the horrible things that happened there? There's a reason we left, you know."

"I know, but how can you call Snow Peak your home when we've lost so many?"

Ella placed a hand on his shoulder. "Home isn't about where you are, or the past. Home is about being safe with people you care about. When you left, you broke up our family."

Alan gazed off. "Yeah. You're completely right." After a long, thoughtful pause, he snapped out of his serious tone and back to his usual self. "So what's the plan?" he asked. "How do we rescue them?"

"What do you mean? You don't have a plan?"

He shrugged and blushed. "Was I supposed to?"

"I guess I should have known better."

"No worries," Rupert said. "We'll think of something right now."

"We can go to the Spire docks," Alan said.

"That place will be swarming with guards," Ella said.

"It wasn't when I was there. Jonah didn't have many guards in the Spire at all. Hell, he may not even know the docks exist. The only reason I know they're there is because of Charlotte."

"Okay, then that's our plan," Ella said. "We dock there and go straight to the armory." She held up the two guns they had. "We're going to need more firepower than this."

"Good idea," Alan said.

"Do you know where to find them?" Ella asked.

He nodded. "They'll either be in the vitality labs, or in Greene's office."

The City wall became visible on the horizon. Alan could just barely see the outline of the Spire. "Over there," he pointed. "That way."

"I see it," Rupert said, steering to the right.

They approached the gate and saw a dozen lights, patrolling back and forth through the docks.

"Crap," Alan said. "The place is full of guards now. It wasn't like that before. It was completely empty when I left."

"They must have noticed the missing boat," Rupert said. "They didn't want you to come back."

"Is there another way in?" Ella asked.

"What about the hole in the outer wall?" Alan suggested. "It's a small entrance. We'll have to abandon the boat completely, but it will put us right by the Spire."

Rupert shook his head and pointed at more guards. "No, look. It's just as bad. That's where Jonah first found us. He knows that's where we'll go."

Ella glanced at Alan. "Is there anywhere else?"

"There's another dock," Alan said, "but it's five miles away. It's where Charlotte brought us last time."

"It sounds like that's our only option," she said.

Alan nodded. "We can't afford to waste any time. Once we dock, we run those five miles. We don't stop."

Rupert steered away from the Spire and headed west.

When they arrived at the Western Gate, they passed between the giant pillars and maneuvered through the cluster of boats. They floated to the end of the dock and carefully bumped against the pier. Alan hopped out first. Ella and Rupert followed his lead.

Ella gazed at the amazing view. "This place is huge," she said. "I can't believe it."

Alan nodded. "I know. I said the same thing. You should see the one at the Spire. It's even bigger." he paused to admire the scene again and then snapped out of it. "Come on, hurry up. We have a lot of ground to cover."

They ran through the streets with scarves pulled over their faces. Alan led them along the same path that Charlotte showed them. It all looked different at night, but the streets were well-lit with lamps, and he could still find his way. People stared briefly at them as they passed by, and then returned to their business. They dashed through intersections and slid through alleyways, making their way toward the Spire.

They turned a corner and hit a tightly packed crowd. Alan turned to find another way, but a swarm of people walked in from behind. They were blocked in. "Not again," Alan said.

"What do we do?" Ella whispered, nervously looking at all of the people.

"We wait for it to clear," Rupert said. "That's all we can do at the moment. We don't want to draw attention to ourselves. Hopefully, it won't be long."

"Hopefully, this time there's no terrorist attack," Alan said.

Ella gave Alan a strange look. She had questions, but decided not to ask. Instead, she poked her head up to peek over the crowd. At the front, she saw a man on a stage. "Who is that?"

Alan popped up to see. It was the man who spoke at the ceremony before the explosions went off. "Oh, him again."

"You know him?" Rupert asked.

"Not personally. I've seen him before. He's their leader, I guess. A supporter of Greene."

The man raised his arms to quiet the chatter. "People. Thank you for coming. This is last minute, I know, but it is of great importance. Most of you know me, but I'll introduce myself anyway. My name is Warren. In the absence of an authority figure, you good people have nominated me to take charge. As you recall, Simon and the Crowns attacked us at our last meeting. Only a true monster would disrupt a memorial like that. In the midst of the attack, they captured Trish Beaumont. They are now holding her as a prisoner. You should already know this, but there's something you may not. More people have gone missing. They've been snatched from their beds in the middle of the night, or in some cases, beaten to submission in broad daylight. Simon is gathering people."

A voice yelled from the back. "He just freed everyone. Why would he capture them again?"

"That is a very good question, and the answer is unclear. Perhaps he still wants something. Maybe he's looking for someone in particular. Regardless, these abductions must be stopped. We will not let his violence scare us. That is why I have formed a plan to take back the Spire. To take control of what's rightfully ours."

Murmurs spread through the crowd.

"Another attack on the Spire?" Ella whispered.

Rupert kept his eyes on the stage. "That's what it sounds like."

"To me, it sounds like they're going to get themselves killed," Alan said.

Ella looked over. "That's what we're doing, isn't it?"

"We're on a rescue mission. We pop in and pop out, hopefully undetected. He's talking a full on attack."

"That's right," Warren continued. "I am working out the details, but sometime tomorrow morning we will charge the Spire. When the sun rises, we march past that wall and take out Simon!"

The crowd cheered on cue as if it were planned.

"I appreciate your enthusiasm. Now, in order for tomorrow to be a success, I need volunteers. Are there people willing to fight?"

Hands shot up all at once. Warren looked over the crowd, satisfied with the response.

"Very good. Please come up, and I will assign tasks."

People shuffled forward. Alan, Ella, and Rupert shimmied through, wiggling from gap to gap. They needed to escape from the cluster. As the movement picked up, the crowd loosened, forming a path to the outside. They dug through the horde and broke free, into an open street.

"Come on," Alan said, following the road.

They moved toward the Spire, and the streets became vacant. No one dared to come so close after Greene's death. They ran ahead until they saw the first wall. To their left was the opening, still in ruins.

They approached the wall and admired its height. They had only seen it from the top of the Spire. From the ground, it looked much bigger. They climbed through the gap, over the debris and bodies. Most of the children had lost any resemblance of identity. Their faces had vanished and turned to ash.

The second wall was not as gruesome. There were no dead children. Just large boulders and the occasional fallen soldier. The third wall was the same. They entered the abandoned lobby, which stood in shambles. It was a place of victory for the Crowns. The wreckage perfectly captured the spirit of their success. It was the first room to greet them as they attacked, and they fully indulged in their victory by trashing the place.

The three of them jogged to the elevator and hit the button. Their first stop was the armory, to stock up on weapons. They rode up to Level 149. The doors opened to a bloody hallway. The smell poured in and slapped them in the face. Ella gagged and immediately covered her nose and mouth.

"It was a slaughter in here," Rupert said. "They didn't even have the decency to clear out the bodies."

"It's Simon we're talking about," Ella said. "Did you really expect him to be decent?"

The stepped out and waded through the soldiers and workers. Ella brushed limbs and heads aside as she walked. Alan was not as careful. He marched along with long strides, kicking everything out of his way.

They reached the supply room and went straight for the gun rack, but it was empty. "Crap!" Alan yelled. "Where the hell are all of the guns?"

"They were likely raided during the attack," Rupert said.

Alan paced back and forth, throwing his arms in the air. "So what do we do now?"

"There must be other armories," Ella said. "We could check the other levels."

Rupert nodded. "That is true, but they will probably be in the same condition. I don't think it's worth checking. We've wasted enough time as it is, and we probably won't find anything."

"So we go in with nothing?" Alan asked.

Ella held up her two weapons. "We still have these."

"That's not enough," Alan said. "He had three guards with him, with more patrolling the hallways, and they're all armed to the teeth."

She handed one of the guns over. "We took out a full group of Greene's men on the boat. We can handle a few of Jonah's men."

Alan grabbed the gun and studied its condition. "We had Charlotte. She handled most of them. We were just a distraction. But now she's gone. We can't handle them on our own."

"It's either that, or we abandon Vince and Izzy."

Alan was torn. Charging in was an option, but they were down an ex-soldier and had less firepower. It would lead to certain death. They had to do something, though. Leaving Vince and Izzy was unacceptable.

"He'll know we're coming," Rupert said. "With all of these cameras, it's impossible to sneak up on him."

Alan's face lit up. "I don't think he knows how to use Greene's system. He had no idea we were coming the last time, and the power to the cell room was still shut off. Either he doesn't care enough to use it, or he doesn't know how. But I do. I watched Charlotte play around with it, and I think I can figure it out. Vince and Izzy are probably locked in the cell room. If we get to the control panel, I can unlock the cells and set them free. I might even be able to hard lock whatever room Jonah is in."

Ella looked at him skeptically. "That is, if he isn't already in Greene's office. If he is, we're screwed."

"It's worth a shot, right? And it's a hell of a lot better than charging in with two guns."

She shrugged. "I suppose."

"If he *is* there, we'll put those two guns to good use before we go down."

Ella smiled. "The things we do for friends, right?"

Alan shook his head. "No. The things we do for family."

"He would do the same for us," Rupert said. "I'm sure of it."

"He already has," Alan said. "He rescued us the day the Spire fell. Now it's time to return the favor."

Ella stepped aside and held out her hand. "Lead the way."

Alan moved toward the door and stopped mid-step. He saw a small box sitting on a table to his right. He reached inside and pulled out an earpiece. "These might come in handy."

TWENTY-SEVEN

VINCE STARED ACROSS the catwalk with Izzy pressed up against his shoulder, thinking of what he would do if they got out alive. Suicide was not an option. He was ashamed to even consider it. Suicide was the coward's way out. Dying as he had lived. In fear.

He considered living in Snow Peak. He had traveled his entire life, never stopping to rest, but now that he had a family, maybe he could finally settle down and live a normal life. He had a place to call home. In the end, home and family were all that mattered.

He also feared Jonah. Not just Jonah, but everyone else like him. There would always be an enemy. Someone so heinous that others would suffer from their actions. There would always be a Barnabus, a Greene, a Simon.

And once Jonah was gone, someone else would take his place. Whoever that may be, Vince would be compelled to stop them. Just another excuse to keep draining. And once they were gone, another would arise. The cycle would never end. He would always have an excuse. These thoughts swam through his head, clouding his mind with doubt.

He heard footsteps coming down the stairs. He gently nudged Izzy and whispered in her ear. "Someone's coming. Stay put." The tap of each step grew louder. A figure hovered into view and peered into the cell.

It stood on the catwalk, at first saying nothing, and reached for the lock around the latch. "Are you two getting nice and comfy in there?" It was Jonah's voice. "Well, too bad. Get up. You're both coming with me." He opened the door and stepped back to let a squad of guards march in. They grabbed Vince and Izzy, tearing them apart. Izzy screamed a screeching cry, kicking her legs to break free, with no success.

"It's okay Izzy," Vince said in the most reassuring voice he could manage. "We'll be okay. I promise."

"Now, don't make any promises you can't keep, Vince," Jonah said as Vince passed by, taking a sip of fresh hot tea from his turtle mug.

He followed behind as the guards dragged them up the stairs. They climbed a few levels and turned off to more cells. Vince saw Trish curled up in one of them. Her lab coat was dirtied with smudges of black, and red. She got to her feet, pushing her glasses up the bridge of her nose, but did not say a word.

Jonah unlocked the cell and stepped back. The guards wrapped her arms behind her and pulled her out. She glared menacingly at Jonah at first, and then shifted her eyes to Vince. Her glare transformed to one of study. She examined his face, gauging his intentions.

They continued up the stairs. No one spoke a word. The only noise was the clang of boots on the metal grating and the occasional sip of tea.

They reached the top and exited the cell room, into the familiar halls of the vitality labs. As they ambled along the path, Vince glanced at Izzy. For the first time, he saw the resemblance to Greene. The rounded cheeks. The piercing eyes. The olive skin with freckles so faint you could barely see them at all. She was the spitting image of Greene. His living legacy.

He moved his eyes to Trish, who was also gazing at Izzy. The girl's indisputable innocence was mesmerizing. She could capture the heart of any soul, if they had one.

"Keep walking, kid," Jonah said with a coarse voice. He nudged her shoulder forward. "It took forever to find this new doctor. I don't want to piss him off by making him wait."

Izzy looked to Trish, and then Vince. There was a clear terror in her eyes, but neither of them could help. Right now, all paths led to death.

They arrived at *Lab No. 88*, and Jonah pointed to the operation room. "Bring them in." He walked over to the desk against the wall, took one final sip of tea, and placed the mug on the wooden surface. Steam danced above the hot liquid.

Vince saw the bloodied body by the door. Its face was blown to pieces, but he still knew who it was. If Charlotte was dead, Alan probably was as well. He looked away until they entered the other room, disgusted by the sight of her corpse, tossed aside without a proper burial.

Jonah joined them in the operation room, and the door slid shut behind him. "Sorry, it's so tight in here. I had to bring more guards, after what happened last time. We don't want that to happen again." He looked down at the streaks of blood on the floor. "Here, let me clean that up," he said, bending over with a damp cloth to wipe it. "There, that's much better." He tossed the rag to the side and held out his hand to shake the doctor's.

The man shook his head. "Sorry, I just sterilized my hands."

Jonah looked at his now bloodied palms. "Huh, I guess the blood soaked through. No worries. I'm glad you could make it up here. You wouldn't believe how hard it is to find someone qualified to do this."

"It's my pleasure. I'd do just about anything for what you're paying me. What's so special about this girl anyway? Why do you need to see her brain?"

"That, sir, is Greene's daughter."

The doctor studied her face. "You don't say."

"It gets better," Jonah said with a smile. "She was created in this lab. Greene grew her from a sample of his own flesh."

"Wow, the things we can do these days. It's amazing."

Jonah nodded. "It sure is. Anyway, her brain has a special mutation that slows her aging. It will help us continue Greene's work. If we can figure out how her unique brain works, we can potentially replicate it in others, and extend the average lifespan twofold. In order to do that, we need to slice open her head."

Izzy backed into a corner and started to cry.

"Oh, don't worry, honey," the doctor said in a comforting tone. "You won't feel a thing. You'll be fast asleep for the whole procedure." He held up a gas mask. "See?" The sight of the mask frightened her more. The doctor shrugged and turned back to Jonah. "Shall we begin?"

"Yes, we shall," Jonah said, motioning to the guards.

They dragged Izzy out of the corner. She screamed, struggling to break free from their grip. Vince and Trish both stepped forward, but the guards raised their guns and forced them back against the door.

Jonah held up his hand. "Don't try anything. The only reason I have you up here is because you two know more about this girl than anyone else. Don't make me regret the decision to let you watch."

The guards threw Izzy onto the table and held down her limbs. The doctor picked up the mask and twisted the metal knobs on the attached tank. A hissing sound leaked from the mask and into the air. He held the mask over her face and slowly lowered it down.

At first, she fought. She twisted and turned, punched and kicked, but the gas was impossible to fight. It seeped through her lips and swam down her lungs. Her movements quickly faded until she could no longer fight. Her eyelids closed and her arms fell peacefully to her sides. The doctor grabbed the scalpel and held it over her forehead.

Vince couldn't bear to watch. He turned away, pushing back against the closed door behind. He peeked to his side to see Trish was doing the same.

The door slid open, and they both fell through. The guards stepped forward to grab them, but the door clamped back down. Vince landed on his back and slid halfway across the floor. He rolled to a crouch and scanned the room with caution, to see Alan standing over him. Relief filled his heart. He got to his feet and pulled Alan in for a hug. "It's so good to see you."

Alan returned the hug. "You too, buddy."

TWENTY-EIGHT

TRISH PICKED HERSELF up off the ground and marveled at the sight of Vince and Alan together. "I can't believe it. Two of the traitors, standing right in front of me."

Alan looked at her curiously. "What?"

They heard Jonah's voice echo from the operation room. His voice was muffled by the thick metal door. "What just happened?" he yelled. "What's going on? Are we locked in here?"

Alan ignored Trish's comment and Jonah's calls. He tuned them out and focused on Vince. "We don't have much time. Izzy's still in there. We need to get her out while they're still confused."

"*I'm* still confused," Vince said. "What's going on?"

Alan pointed first to his ear piece, and then to a camera on the wall. "Rupert and Ella. They're watching us."

Jonah started to pound on the door. "Why won't this damn thing open? Is the key card broken?"

Alan handed an extra earpiece to Vince. He took it and immediately dug it into his ear.

"Hurry up guys," he could hear Ella say. "You're running out of time."

"What do we do?" Vince asked, looking at Alan.

He shrugged. "We don't really have a plan."

"You don't have a plan?" Vince repeated.

"We were in a rush. I tried to get down here as fast as I could."

The banging on the door stopped. "Forget it," Jonah said. "We don't need them. Doctor, continue with the—Crap! Not now."

"What's happening?" Alan asked.

Ella replied in his ear. "It's Izzy. She's having another seizure. It looks like she just bought you some time. Make the most of it."

"I can't continue while she's like this," the doctor said. "We'll have to wait for the seizure to pass." He put down the scalpel and stepped away from the table.

"Wait a minute," Ella said. "The doctor, he's moving towards the door."

"So what?" Alan asked.

"So grab him. They can't do the surgery without the doctor. I'll open the door, and you yank him out. I'll lock the door again, and Jonah will be trapped inside."

"What about Izzy?" Alan said. "She'll be trapped in there too."

"She's not in any danger. They need to keep her alive for the surgery. It will at least buy us some time."

Alan looked at Vince with immense skepticism. "And what if it doesn't work? What if you open that door and he shoots us on sight?"

"Look, we don't have time to argue. Her seizure only lasts a couple minutes. After that, they go on with the surgery. This is our best option. He's in the perfect position, right where Vince was standing, in front of the door. Just be quick. They're not even paying attention. I'll shut the door before they even know what's going on."

"She's right," Vince said. "It's our only option. We should take advantage of this opportunity."

"Fine," Alan sighed, "but you better be fast."

"Don't worry," Ella said. "That door will be shut in no time."

Alan walked up and got ready, bending his knees and extending his arms. Vince joined him and did the same.

"Okay," Ella said. "He is standing about two feet from the door. A little to the right. On three, I'll open the door."

Alan nodded. "We're ready."

"One. Two. Three!"

The door slid open. Alan and Vince reached inside and grabbed the doctor's shoulders. They pulled back, tumbling onto their backs and smacking down hard on the floor. Jonah turned his head and the guards raised their guns, but the door slammed shut before they could get a shot.

Jonah pounded the door again. "Hey! Open up! I need him! Goddamn it!"

"We got him," Alan said to Ella, getting to his feet and dusting himself off. "Now what?"

"We can use him as leverage," she said.

Alan glanced at the doctor, who was still recovering from the fall. "How? Jonah's not going to give up the girl. That's the whole reason he needs this guy in the first place. He can't perform surgery without Izzy."

Ella had no answer. They stood in silence, not sure how to proceed. Vince wandered to the wooden desk, where he found his bag hanging from the chair. He grabbed it and strapped it over his shoulder. He studied the turtle mug sitting on the desk, full of hot tea, while the others considered their options.

"Give me my doctor back!" Jonah yelled.

Trish, who had stood aside and watched, stepped forward. "You could suffocate them."

"What?" Alan asked.

"Suck out all of the air." She pointed to his earpiece. "Whoever you're talking to has control, right?"

Alan nodded.

"So suck out the air."

"What do you mean?"

"It was installed to extinguish fires. If there is an isolated fire, all of these rooms are airtight. If you suck out the air, the fire goes out."

"But Izzy's in there," Alan said.

"It won't kill them. For safety, it's on a timer. The vacuum only lasts twenty seconds, but that should be enough to knock them out. It's hard locked for an hour after you activate it, so we only get one shot."

The doctor backed away. "This is nuts," he said. "I'm out of here. That sucker already paid me anyway." He ran out the door.

"We don't need him," Vince said, touching the rim of the turtle mug and wandering back. "You're sure this will work?"

"Yes. I know you've just met me, and you probably don't trust me. You have good reason not to. I've been calling you traitors this whole time. I don't know what you're up to, but we both seem to want the same thing. To get that girl out safely. Am I correct?"

Vince and Alan nodded.

"Okay, then traitors or not, let's get her out. Let's suck out all of that air."

Alan glanced at Vince. "That's good enough for me. Did you hear that, Ella?"

"Every word," she said. "How do I do it?"

Alan removed his earpiece and handed it to Trish. "Here, walk her through it."

She grabbed it and pressed it into her ear. "Are you in the Spire database?"

"Uhh, I think so."

"You see the camera view of this room, right?"

"Yes."

"Okay, so you have access to this room. If you go back to the main directory for Vitality Lab No. 88, there should be an option labeled *emergency override*."

"Hold on." There were a series of clicks as Ella stumbled through the menus. "Okay, I found it."

"Select *fire*."

"Okay. The options are *sprinklers* and *vacuum*."

"Good. Vacuum is what we want. Let us get ready before you activate it." She turned the Vince and Alan. "Once the twenty seconds are up, the door will automatically open. When that happens, you can pop in and grab Izzy. Everyone will be knocked out, so it should be a piece of cake."

"Are you ready?" Ella asked.

Vince and Alan nodded.

"Yes, we're ready," Trish answered.

"Here we go."

The three of them stood by the door, listening to the sounds from inside. They heard the rumble of a vent. It grew to a loud roar, whirring with intense ferocity, and then immediately stopped.

"What's that?" Jonah said, with concern in his tone. His voice grew raspy as he spoke, and he started to cough and pant. The guards did the same. "Hey! Let us out!" he yelled, pounding on the door.

They heard many sounds as they waited. Guns clanging on the tile floor. Desperate wheezing. Hopeless clawing against the walls. One body dropping. Then another.

Alan looked intently at the clock against the wall, counting down the twenty seconds. "Will it be enough to knock all of them out?" he asked.

"It should be," Trish answered, watching the clock as well.

Another body dropped. And another.

"Twenty seconds is almost up," Trish said. "Get ready." They moved closer to the door, ready to charge in.

The door slid open, and a loud pop blasted their ears. A strong force sucked them forward into the room. They slammed into Jonah, and flew across the room, hitting the opposite wall and falling to the ground. The push of air ripped Izzy from the table, tearing the mask from her face and sending her into flight.

Vince rolled over and oriented himself, getting to his feet. He ran for Izzy, passing by Jonah, who was gasping for air. Trish and Alan jumped to their feet and kicked the guards who were squirming on the floor.

Vince bent down and held Izzy in his arms, carrying her like his own child. "I have her," he said, nodding to the others. "Come on, let's go."

They nodded and jogged to the exit, with Vince following behind. Jonah leaped through the air and grabbed Vince's foot. Vince nearly fell, but managed to keep his balance.

"You're not going anywhere with that girl," Jonah said.

Vince shook his leg, but Jonah's grip was too tight. Alan charged back and kicked Jonah square in the jaw. Jonah let go and rolled onto his back. Alan glanced at Vince. "Let's get the hell out of here."

They ran through the door and into the hallway. Trish seemed to know her way through the maze. She led them to the main corridor, and back to the elevators. They eagerly waited for the lift to arrive, glancing over their shoulders with a paranoid sense of urgency. The doors slid opened to the sight of Ella and Rupert, standing side by side. Ella smiled. "It's good to see you, Vince." They entered, and Trish pushed *Level 0*.

Alan shook his head. "Not the docks. They're swimming with guards." He reached out and pressed *Level 1* instead.

They rode down and came out to a deserted lobby. Vince found the emptiness disturbing. The last time he had seen the lobby, it was full of angry Crowns storming up the Spire. The stark contrast was somehow both calming and haunting at the same time.

They pushed through the front doors to the outside. The sky glowed a fiery orange as the sun began to rise. They climbed over debris to get through the walls and into the streets.

"Thank you for your help," Trish said. "Now, would you like to explain why you're helping this girl?"

"What do you mean?" Vince asked.

"You betrayed Greene. You stabbed him in the back and went to work for Simon. You know who this girl is, right?"

Vince reached into his bag and pulled out the monitor journal. "She's Greene's daughter."

She tilted her head, now even more confused. "Right. So why did you kill Simon? Why did you save her?"

"We were never working for Simon," he said. "We were never working for Greene, either. We were only trying to survive, and both of them wanted us dead.

"Why are you trying to save her?" Alan asked. "Jonah is continuing his work in the labs. Isn't that what you want?"

"We didn't want *this*. Yes, we plan on starting up the tests again, but we have limits. We follow Greene's principles. One of those principles was no children, especially not this one."

Alan chuckled at the idea of Greene having principles.

"He kept Izzy alive for a reason," she continued. "We intend to do the same."

"But you *do* wish to continue the tests," Vince said with a stern face.

"We do. The tests are the reason the City thrives. They must go on."

Alan opened his mouth to argue, but Vince held up his hand and spoke first. "Very well. It seems we have had a misunderstanding. I think our goals align."

The others stared at Vince with shock. He had been so adamantly against the tests, that it was strange to hear him praise them.

Trish nodded. "Hmm. It seems so."

Vince looked into Izzy's face as she slept in his arms. "How long do you think she'll be out?" he asked.

"That stuff they gave her is pretty strong," Trish said. "And they gave her a lot. It should wear off in ten minutes or so, though she will be pretty weak. It will be a few hours before she fully recovers."

Rupert pointed to Vince's leg. "Vince, you're bleeding."

He looked down to see a scalpel sticking out of his thigh. In the chaos, he had not noticed the stray blade wedge into his skin. He handed Izzy to Rupert and grabbed the handle of the blade, yanking it out in one swift motion. Blood slowly oozed out. He untied his scarf from his neck and wrapped it around the wound. "I'll live," he said.

As Rupert handed her back, a voice came from down the street. "Trish?" It was a man with a familiar face.

"Warren," Trish said, walking over to greet him.

He searched up and down her body, looking for scratches or bruises. "You got out."

She nodded. "I didn't do it alone. I had help."

Warren glanced at the group behind her and leaned in. "Don't you recognize these people?" he whispered. "They're the traitors from Snow Peak."

"They're on our side. They saved me. And they saved that girl's life."

"Who is the girl?"

"She's very important." She turned around and held out her hand. "Vince, pass me the journal."

Vince handed it over, and she gave it to Warren. He flipped through the pages. "Project Monika?"

"Read through it and you'll know why she's so important."

He clamped the book shut. "Later. There's no time right now. We're about to charge into the Spire."

She furrowed her brow. "You're attacking?"

He nodded. "Ever since you were taken, more and more people have gone missing. Simon has them."

"Simon's dead," she said.

"What?"

She pointed to Vince. "He killed him. He's gone. Now Jonah's in charge."

"Jonah? Simon's grunt?"

"That's right," she said. "He turned on Simon and has been gathering labbies and test subjects."

Alan slapped his forehead. "We're idiots," he said. "Jonah was on the ground. Incapacitated. We could have killed him and ended it all."

Vince smiled.

"What are you grinning about?" Alan asked. He saw Vince's hand press against his empty pocket and figured it out on him own. "Ha! Vince, you sneaky bastard. You slipped that pill into his tea, didn't you? That fool's a sucker for tea. He probably took a big sip the second he got up."

Vince answered with an even wider grin.

"What does that mean?" Warren asked.

Vince finally broke his silence. "He will be dead by the time you get up there."

"That will make it easier for your attack," Trish said. "They have no leader. They'll be lost in confusion."

Warren nodded. "Good. We'll need all the help we can get. Rumor has it the Crowns are charging the Spire as well. We thought that perhaps they were preparing for our attack. We wanted to make our move before they could get back, but now it's clear they're not after us. They want Jonah."

"Man," Alan said, "it's going to be a mess up there. Jonah's men, Simon's men, and now you guys?"

"At least they'll be occupied," Rupert said, looking down at Izzy. "Jonah's men will be too busy to come after her."

"Leave her with me," Trish said. "I'll bring her back to our base. She'll be safe there."

Rupert shook his head. "She'll be safest in Snow Peak, away from the City."

Vince nodded. "Yes. She comes with us."

"But the people need to know about her. You read the journal. It's what Greene wanted."

"That may be true," Vince said, "but it's not what's best for her. She doesn't belong here. She never chose this life. She deserves a level of safety that you can't offer."

"But—"

"Take the monitor journal," he interrupted. "Show the people his last written words. Show them the miracle that Izzy represents. Do whatever you want with that journal, but do not tell them where we are. Doing so will only make things worse."

"So what do I say happened to her? They are going to want to see her."

Alan stepped forward, growing impatient with her questions. "You could tell them she's dead for all I care. Make something up. They don't need to know. Greene's word will still get to the people. Hell, you can turn her into a martyr. Make her the face of your resistance. The people will eat that up."

She pondered the idea of creating an image for the resistance. "I suppose that's an option, but you don't have to leave. Stay and help us fight. Your presence will inspire them even more. You're the ones responsible for Simon and Jonah's deaths, after all."

"No," Vince said. "We're done with this place. It's time for us to go home."

"But you could help. You could make such a big difference. Don't you want the world to be a better place?"

"I've spent my whole life making the world a better place," he said. "Now it's time for me to rest. We've all earned a little rest."

Trish looked sternly in his eyes and saw she would not persuade him. "Very well. Good luck to all of you."

They exchanged one last look and parted ways. Trish and Warren walked towards the Spire. Vince, Ella, Alan, and Rupert walked towards the Western Gate.

"What you said back there," Alan said, "you didn't really mean it, did you? You don't want the tests to continue."

"Of course not, but it's no longer our business. We're together and safe. That's all that matters."

"You're not going to try to stop them anymore?"

"No."

Alan's face held puzzled curiosity. "But that was the reason we came here in the first place."

"Do you think they'll succeed?" Ella asked. People ran past them on both sides, following Warren's lead. "Do you think they can take back the Spire?"

"They have a good chance," Rupert said. "There may be a lot of troops up there, but with Simon and Jonah gone, they'll be disorganized."

"I suppose it doesn't matter," Ella said. "For us, anyway. Soon we'll be back in Snow Peak, away from this whole mess."

Alan kicked a pebble along the road. "What about you, Vince? Do you think they'll succeed?"

Vince kept his gaze straight ahead as he spoke. "I don't know, and I suppose I don't care. Ella is right. It's no longer our business."

"If they take it back, they'll start up the tests again," Alan said. "You're okay with that?"

"There's one thing I've learned from our time in the City. There will always be a bad guy. Whether it's Barnabus, or Greene, or Simon, or Jonah, it will never stop. If we eliminate one, another will rise in his spot. I once thought it was my job to stop them, but now I realize that chasing the cycle is not a job for one man. There will always be monsters in the world, but there will always be someone to fight them, as well. Someone will rise up in Jonah's place. And someone will rise up in mine. Someone who will stand up for those who can't defend themselves and resist the evil that plagues this world. Just like the cycle for bad, there is a cycle for good. I've done my part in the world. Now it's time to pass it off to whoever is next."

"Tag team," Izzy said, her eyes barely opening as she slowly regained consciousness.

Vince looked down at her face and smiled. "Yes. Tag team."

Dozens of Spire workers ran past them, towards the Spire, as part of a movement to take back what was theirs. The new rebels in a chaotic age. The age of Greene had ended, the age of Simon was gone, and the short-lived age of Jonah would soon perish as well. In its place, a new age would rise, and just like everything else, it would eventually end. It was a cycle. An age of end.

EPILOGUE

ELLA GRABBED THE mug of hot tea and touched the rim to her lips. The liquid was still scalding hot, so she placed it back down to cool. Her aged face was still vibrant and beautiful. She tapped her finger against her knee, waiting for the last of their party to arrive.

Rupert sat across from her, stroking his thick beard, which was sprinkled with flecks of white. His shoulder stood absent of Snow Peak's beloved falcon. Fred had passed on years ago. Rupert gazed out the window at the neighbors trudging through the snow. It had been a tough ten-year transition, but the Spire folk had finally adapted to their new home. They had built a community that was just as strong as before.

Alan entered the cabin, bundled up in a large coat and scarf. He stomped the snow from his feet and stripped off his layers, hanging his wet clothes on the hook by the door. "It sure is cold out there," he said. "Izzy will be here soon. She said to give her five minutes." He gazed down at Vince, who was lying peacefully in bed, covers pulled up to his chin, with his eyes closed. "How is he doing?" he asked.

"He's still with us," Ella said. "He's just resting his eyes."

Alan took a seat by the bed, taking Vince's hand and glancing into his face. It was pale and full of wrinkles. "She's on her way, buddy," he said and looked to Ella. "How long has he been out?"

"Not long," she said. "Only a few minutes." She reached for her tea to take a bigger sip this time.

Rupert raised his own mug to find that it was empty. "I could use some more tea. Alan, do you want some? You look cold."

Alan nodded. "Please."

Rupert got up and exited to the kitchen.

"How's the kid?" Alan asked.

"He's a handful, but I love every minute of it. He's growing up so fast. It feels like just yesterday I was rocking him in my arms. Now he's always running about. He's a little ball of energy."

"Time does fly, doesn't it?"

She nodded. "It sure does. What about you? I haven't seen you in a while. How are things?"

"Things are good. Trevor's a handful, but the man sure can hunt. It's funny. He was the laziest guy in the Spire, and now he's one of the hardest workers in Snow Peak. He's really changed."

"I think we've all changed."

Alan looked down at Vince's pale skin. "How do you think she'll handle, you know, seeing him like this?"

"It will be hard on her, for sure, but she's a tough girl. She'll be okay."

"Vince brought her up well. She speaks just like him. She's a little reserved, but has a strong will. She's grown into a woman who can handle herself. But even the strongest of us have weak moments."

"Of course, she'll be shaken," Ella said, "but so will I. All of us will be shaken. He is a great man who has done great things in his life. That will never change. I will miss him dearly, but in time, we will all learn to live without him, her included."

Rupert reentered from the kitchen with a full cup of tea in each hand. He passed one to Alan and sat back down. "Careful," he said. "It's hot." He blew on the surface, watching the steam dance away.

Alan brought the tea to his lips and took a larger sip than he expected. The liquid scorched his tongue and throat. "Jeez, that's hot!"

"You never learn," Rupert said.

Alan lifted his mug with a nod. "And I never will."

The front door swung open, and a tall woman walked in. Her golden hair shined with the sun as she flipped back her hood. Her skin was smooth and radiant. She took off her coat and hung it next to Alan's. "Is he awake yet?"

"Not yet," Rupert answered. "He's still resting. Take a seat, Izzy."

She walked across the room and pulled a chair next to Ella.

"Tea?" Rupert offered, holding up his mug.

"No, thank you." She stared at Vince. At his face. His dry hair. His closed eyes. His wrinkled skin.

"Are you okay?" Ella asked.

Izzy sniffled. "Yes, I'm fine."

Vince rolled his head to the side and slowly opened his eyes. He blinked as his dry pupils adjusted to the strong sunlight. A deep breath filled his lungs and released all at once. His cracked lips trembled with the slightest bit of movement. The four of them stood and gathered around the bed.

"Hey, Vince," Alan said. "How are you feeling?"

Vince managed a smile at the sight of his friends. He opened his mouth, trying to speak, but his throat was too dry. He coughed and wheezed, and then spoke a single word. "Family," he said. His voice was low and raspy.

"That's right," Alan said. "We're all here. And there's nowhere else we'd rather be."

"Good," he said. His voice got softer as he spoke. "I want to say something to each of you."

They all leaned forward, waiting with patience. They did not want to interrupt what would likely be his last words.

"Rupert," Vince whispered. "You're a good man. You are genuine and kind. You have a warm soul. You were the first to welcome me into your community, and you've supported me along the way. Through every hardship, every difficult decision, you helped guide my way. I thank you for being a good leader, and a great friend."

Rupert accepted his words with a stern nod.

"Ella." His voice was even fainter now. "You are a strong woman. You always have been. And you have always valued family. That is something I admire. Your loved ones always come first. You put their needs ahead of your own. That kind of selflessness inspires me. It gives me hope that there are others like you out in the world. I have no doubt, your son will grow up to do great things."

She flashed a sad smile.

"Alan. There's so much good to say. You are the happiest man I have ever met. No matter how bad things get, you always manage to find a laugh. You lift people's spirits when they are at their worst. Your presence spreads happiness. That is a valuable gift. Don't ever give it up. The world needs people like you."

A single tear ran down Alan's cheek, and he quickly wiped it away.

"And Izzy." Vince's voice was so soft they could just barely hear him now. He waved her in to come closer. "You have grown up so much. You're so mature now. So smart."

She sniffled again, her face glazed with tears. "I got that all from you," she said.

"And you will spread it to others." He reached for her hand. She held it out and let him grip her fingers. "I am so proud of you. You're like the daughter I never had."

She gently shook her head. "No. I *am* your daughter."

He grinned. "That's right. I can no longer change the world. That is up to you now."

"Tag team," she whispered.

He nodded. "Tag team." His voice trailed off and his eyes closed.

They all stood around the bed and watched an immortal man die. He was a man who had once feared death, but eventually learned to embrace his fate. Surrounded by family, Vince perished peacefully into the unknown, ready to join Saul and Charlotte, wherever they might be. His endless cycle was broken at last, and in his place, Izzy would rise.

THE END

Want More?

For news on upcoming books, sign up for Moon Mail at:

www.tothemoonpublish.com/moon-mail

Did you leave a review?

Written reviews greatly help a book get noticed. If you enjoyed this book and would like to help me out, please leave a review and let others know about the series. Thank you for supporting me!

About The Author:

Chris Yee grew up in Needham, Massachusetts. As a young child, he had a wild imagination, thinking up stories of mystery and wonder. People would ask what he wanted to be when he grew up, and the answer was always the same. He wanted to be an author. As he grew older, educational interests pulled him away from the world of writing and into math and science. He attended Northeastern University and received a Bachelor's Degree in civil engineering. He now works in Boston, full-time as an engineer. Despite his technical background, he never lost an interest in writing. He writes every day, to fulfill a passion that has never faded.